THE BEWILDERED BRIDE

Margaret had thought herself the happiest of young ladies when the Earl of Brampton asked her to be his wife. For years she had secretly adored this handsome lord, and now she would have her fondest dreams fulfilled.

Yet on the morning after her wedding night, Margaret lay alone and afraid there had been a terrible mistake.

It wasn't that her bridegroom had hurt her. On the contrary, he had been most respectful—if not clearly indifferent—as he did his duty in officially making her his wife.

If this was all that their marriage meant to the Earl, Margaret concluded, he surely was going to search for someone else with whom to share his pleasure . . . and she was determined that she would be the one he found. . . .

A MASKED DECEPTION

More Delightful Regency Romances from SIGNET

A MASKED DECEPTION

Mary Balogh

A SIGNET BOOK

NEW AMERICAN LIBRARY

NAL Books are available at quantity discounts when used
to promote products or services. For information please write to
Premium Marketing Division, New American Library,
1633 Broadway, New York, New York 10019

Signet, Signet Classic, Mentor, Plume, Meridian, and NAL Books
are published by New American Library
1633 Broadway, New York, New York 10019

First Printing, February, 1985

1   2   3   4   5   6   7   8   9

PRINTED IN THE UNITED STATES OF AMERICA

1

Richard Adair, seventh Earl of Brampton, was not quite sure whether he was feeling just uncomfortable or actually bored. Neither was a feeling he usually allowed himself to be trapped into. He lifted the delicate china teacup to his lips, only to discover that it was empty. He set it down in the saucer and placed both on the table beside his chair.

He looked across the drawing room to his companion, who appeared to be quite comfortably engrossed in her embroidery. His eyes traveled with some distaste to the little lace cap that she wore on her brown hair, which was drawn smoothly back from her face and coiled in heavy braids at the back. How old was she, for God's sake? Brampton wondered irritably. Twenty-six? Twenty-seven? She behaved as if she were a maiden aunt in her dotage.

His eyes wandered over the placid face, eyes lowered to her work, surprisingly long, dark lashes fanning pale cheeks, the straight, short nose, a mouth that could be described as sweet, but was certainly not inviting. Would one call her face heart-shaped? he wondered idly. Or was that glamorizing it too much?

He watched the rise and fall of her slight breasts, which were flattered by the high waistline of her blue muslin day dress. He looked at her little feet, set neatly side by side in their dark-blue slippers. Altogether, he concluded silently and bluntly, she was not much of a prize.

Margaret Wells paused in her work and raised her eyes to his. He was jolted back to reality, suddenly aware of his ill-mannered silence.

"What do you hear of your brothers, my lord?" she asked, her voice low and melodic, but totally lacking in the type of inflection that could capture his interest.

"My mother received a letter from him just one week ago," he replied. "He is still in Spain, enduring the rain and the mud and the constant marches from place to place, but so far has escaped injury."

"I am pleased to hear that, my lord," she commented.

And that exhausted that topic, he decided gloomily.

He drew a deep breath and finally got to the point of his visit. "Miss Wells," he began, crossing one elegantly booted leg over the other, "you must know, I believe, that I have spoken with your father and received his permission to pay my addresses to you. You would be doing me a great honor if you would consent to become my wife."

He kept his eyes steadily on the little figure seated on the sofa opposite him. Her eyes stayed on the embroidery, but her hands had stilled.

"Yes, my lord, I did know the reason for your visit," Margaret replied, her voice quite calm. "You mistake, sir. The honor is all mine. I shall be happy to accept your proposal."

She looked up at him again, and once more he felt jolted. Those gray eyes certainly did not belong with the plain and placid little person that was Margaret

Wells. They almost made him forget that she was not at all beautiful.

Brampton shifted uncomfortably in his chair. Now what? He had not thought beyond the terrible ordeal of the proposal. He got to his feet and bowed formally.

"You have made me a happy man, Miss Wells," he lied. "I am afraid that we have not yet had a chance to become well acquainted, but I believe that we shall deal well together. I have spoken with your mother, and she has agreed to allow me to escort the two of you to the opera this evening. I believe that her sister and your uncle will make up the party."

Margaret murmured her thanks, quietly set aside her needlework, and rose to her feet. She looked up into his face from the vantage point of somewhere on a level with his broad shoulders accentuated by a tight-fitting and immaculately tailored coat of green superfine.

"Until this evening, then, Miss Wells," Brampton said. "Good afternoon to you." He reached for her hand and raised it to his lips.

"Good afternoon, my lord," Margaret replied, dropping him a deep curtsy.

Eleven hours later, at two o'clock in the morning to be exact, the Earl of Brampton sat alone in the library of his town house in Grosvenor Square, getting slowly but very effectively drunk. The brandy decanter beside him was all but empty; another stood on the desk, waiting to be tackled. Chalmer, the butler, and Stevens, Brampton's valet, had both been sent to bed and ordered not to disturb him again that night.

"So," he said aloud to his brandy glass, peering

through the clear liquid to the dancing flames of the log fire a few feet away, "at the grand age of thirty-three, you are getting leg-shackled, are you, Brampton? You are giving up all the loneliness and cheerlessness of a bachelor home for the bliss of matrimony—and with an antidote like Margaret Wells, self-styled spinster who was unable to snare a husband in more than five Seasons in London, until she gave up the struggle and donned her old maid's cap."

He laughed harshly, reached out with one foot to push a log back into the blaze, and lurched to his feet. A few moments later he gazed with satisfaction at a full glass of brandy and stumbled back to his chair.

"And with this paragon of beauty and feminine grace and charm," he continued, still aloud, "you are proposing to set up your nursery." He shuddered with distaste at the fashionable phrase which always conjured up in his mind unpleasant images of squawking babies and nursemaids.

Brampton drank down his brandy as he would a glass of water on a hot day. He let his head fall back against the comfortable headrest of his favorite leather chair. A curse on all mothers and sisters, he thought with weary venom, and closed his eyes.

He was back in his mother's drawing room a week before. A note summoning him there had been awaiting him when he returned home from a morning visit to Tattersall's, where he had been trying to close a deal for the purchase of a pair of matched grays for his new curricle.

Brampton knew that he did not visit his mother as often as he should. He had all the affection in the world for her, but was very aware that she had a one-track mind. Marriage seemed to be the only topic that really animated her and gave her the energy to get up in the morning and live through the day. Up to two years ago, the situation had been tolerable. There had been three daughters to bring out and get suitably matched. That task had been finally accomplished three years before, when Brampton's youngest sister, Lucy, had married Sir Henry Wood at the age of nineteen.

For one year after the marriage of her daughter, Lady Brampton had only occasionally nagged her older son to choose a wife and settle down; her younger son, Charles, had still been at home. Then Charles had persuaded his brother to buy him a commission in the army and had gone adventuring to Spain to fight Bonaparte's troops. Lady Brampton had stepped up the campaign against Richard.

It had reached its climax during that afternoon visit a week before. Brampton had known she meant business as soon as he saw Rosalind, the oldest of his sisters, firmly ensconced in the chair next to the hearth. Rosalind had always been considered the "sensible" one. All that meant was that she was prosy and totally lacked a sense of humor. She had obviously been installed as moral support.

It had not taken his mother many minutes to come to the point. It was time he put behind him his wild ways (someone had obviously told her of his latest mistress, then) and took a wife; he was the head of the family and should take it upon himself to set a good example to the other members; it was high time that he secured the succession by setting up his nursery (he had winced); dear Charles could be killed any day and then the future of the family would look very bleak, everything depending upon dear Richard;

and—the crowning detail of her argument—how would he enjoy seeing Cousin Osbert succeed to the title, the property, and the fortune?

Brampton refrained from pointing out that he was never likely to see any such thing, since he would have to be dead before Osbert could succeed—supposing, of course, that Charles were also dead. He crossed one leg over the other and stared gloomily at his left foot, jiggling it slightly so that the tassels of his gleaming Hessians swung back and forth.

"Really, Richard dear, you should consider poor Mama's feelings," Rosalind had added, "if she were to be ousted from her home by my upstart cousin."

Brampton had blinked. His mother lived in a very comfortable house on Curzon Street, left her quite unentailed in her husband's will. He had wisely refrained from pointing out this fact. He had stood up and wandered restlessly to the window that overlooked the busy street outside.

"Very well, Mama," he had said at last, abruptly. "I have been aware of my responsibility for some time now. Unfortunately, I have no candidates for wife in mind. Do you?" He had swung around and favored his mother with a piercing glance from his blue eyes.

She had picked up her cue without hesitation. "Well, there's Melissa Rathb—"

"Not a simpering miss from Almack's," Brampton had cut in. "Spare me that, Mama."

"Well, she is rather silly, and her conversation is not highly edifying," Rosalind had commented, unexpectedly coming to her brother's defense.

"Then how about Nora Denning? She has beauty, wealth, position . . ."

"No!" Brampton had thundered. "If I want an iceberg, I shall join a naval expedition to the North."

"Really, my dear, I do believe she would make an excellent countess," Lady Brampton had urged.

"Perhaps so, Mama, but she will not be *my* countess," her son had answered firmly.

"You are being very unreasonable, my love," Lady Brampton had complained.

Rosalind had reached into her reticule and withdrawn her vinaigrette, glaring meaningfully at her brother. "There is always Margaret Wells," she had said.

Brampton had laughed. "Yes, I suppose there is always Margaret Wells," he had agreed.

"Really, Richard," Rosalind had continued crossly, "she is a very respectable female. It is true that she never really took with the *ton*, but I do believe it was her good sense and proper manner that frightened away any would-be suitors. She would make an eminently suitable wife, I am sure. True, her father is neither titled nor wealthy, but he is of impeccable lineage and manages to maintain a country estate as well as a town house. I hear they are even planning a Season for the younger girl, Charlotte."

"Margaret Wells. Is she the sweet little lady who has taken to sitting with the chaperones at assemblies? And has donned caps?" Lady Brampton had asked.

And somehow, he was never to know quite how, Brampton had found himself drawn inextricably into the scheme. Lady Brampton had renewed her old acquaintance with Mrs. Wells; the Earl of Brampton had joined a card table at White's Club with Mr. Wells one evening and had waited on him the next day to propose a marriage contract with his daughter.

Brampton, reclining now in his library, raised his

glass to his eye. Strange! Brandy was dark brown, was it not, not transparent? And when you turned the glass upside down, was not the liquid supposed to pour out? His sluggish brain finally reached the inevitable conclusion: the glass must be empty! "At least I am not quite drunk," he sighed with relief as he pulled himself out of his chair and tried to steer the shortest course to the desk. The glass refilled, Brampton somehow found his way back to the sanctuary of the chair and sank into it.

Well, the deed was done. He was affianced, and according to the code of gentlemanly ethics by which he lived, there was no possible way of turning back now. He was doomed to having that dull and unattractive woman living permanently in his home. He was going to have to visit her bed regularly each night. I shall have to hope that she proves fertile and I potent, he thought in despair. Once she begins to increase, at least I shall be spared that ordeal. Until the next time around, that is.

His thoughts passed sluggishly, but by a natural progression, to Lisa. He wished that he had not drunk so much. It might have helped now to drive to the little house in which he had set her up three months ago in a discreet area of London, and bury his sorrows and misgivings in her soft and ample and very feminine body. He thought longingly of her thick, blond hair and her tantalizingly rouged cheeks and full lips, of her heavy breasts, narrow waist, and ample hips, of her nimble, roving fingers.

He dragged his mind away. Not tonight! He could not even drag up enough desire to make the thought process worthwhile. At least in the future he would have Lisa to satisfy his sexual appetite while duty forced him to use his wife to procure the succession.

Brampton's head drooped. He began to snore

heavily at about the same moment as his half-filled brandy glass slipped from his nerveless fingers and spilled its contents over his library carpet.

Margaret Wells was still awake. She had retired to her room as soon as Lord Brampton had returned her and her mother to their home after the opera. Kitty, her lady's maid, had undressed her, brushed and braided her hair, brought her a cup of steaming chocolate, and snuffed the candles before she left. For a couple of hours Margaret had tossed and turned, trying to still her churning thoughts, trying to induce sleep. But by now she had accepted the fact that she would not sleep, and lay quietly on her back, hands propped behind her head on the pillow, staring at the rust-colored velvet hangings above her head.

She was not quite sure whether she was in the middle of a rapturous dream or a ghastly nightmare. All she did know was that suddenly, with only one day's warning, she was betrothed to the man she had loved passionately and hopelessly for six years. Her mind could still not grasp the fact as reality. When Papa had warned her the day before that Richard Adair, Earl of Brampton, was to come the next day to pay his addresses to her, Margaret had felt a sick lurching of her stomach. How had her father discovered her feelings? What sort of a sick joke was he playing on her?

And when she had sat across from the earl that afternoon, she had had to use all her willpower to put into practice the training of her youth—to sit quietly poised before him, not betraying her feelings by so much as a tremble in her hands or a softening of her lips. But she had had to look up at him now and again to convince herself that he really was

there. She had not needed the evidence of her eyes
when he had taken her hand in his. All her feelings
had come to the fire and she had had great difficulty
controlling her voice when his lips had brushed her
hand for a brief moment.

Margaret had had a quiet childhood and a strict
upbringing. Her father was not a wealthy man. He
had kept his family at his estate in Leicestershire
most of the time, taking them to London only
occasionally. Her mother was a quiet and sober
woman; she had instilled these virtues in her
daughter. When Margaret's only sister had been
born seven years after her, Margaret had been
expected even more to set an example as the older
sister. And she had learned her lesson well. No one
knew, except perhaps Charlotte, who loved her sister
so deeply that she saw beyond the outer facade, that
Margaret was a woman with passion and deep
feelings, who longed to be gay and adventurous. All
signs of the real Margaret were fiercely repressed.

Her parents had taken her to London for her come-
out when she was eighteen. Although not wealthy,
Mr. Wells was accepted unquestioningly by the *ton;*
Margaret, therefore, had soon been caught up in the
whirl of balls, routs, soirees, and other entertain-
ments with which the *ton* occupied their time. And
she had loved every moment of it. Although her
public image was the quiet one which she had been
trained to project, she had not lacked either for
female friends or for male admirers. She had not
exactly taken the *ton* by storm, but her trim little
figure, her heart-shaped face with the large, quiet
gray eyes framed by long, dark lashes, and her sweet
mouth had made her a pleasing attraction.

That had all been before the night of the Hetheringtons' masquerade ball, two months after her

come-out. The chance to attend a masquerade was rare; the regular masquerade balls held at the opera house were considered unsuitable for the girls of the *ton*. They were noisy, rather ribald affairs. Consequently, invitations to the Hetheringtons' ball had been coveted and the event had developed into a great squeeze. Fortunately, the day had been unseasonably warm for April. The garden had been decked with lanterns so that the crowd had been able to spill out into the outdoors away from the stuffy ballroom.

Margaret had been dressed as Marie Antoinette, her wide-skirted silver dress and powdered wig hired for the occasion, a silver mask covering her whole face except her eyes, mouth, and jawline. She had been excited. Somehow, knowing that she was disguised almost beyond recognition, she had felt as if she could throw away the restraints that were normally second nature to her. She had danced and laughed and talked, lowering the tone of her voice and assuming a French accent. Her behavior had become even more animated when she had realized that both her mother and her father had disappeared into the card room.

And then she had seen the Earl of Brampton. He had been unmistakable, his tall, broad-shouldered figure clothed in a black domino, a glimpse of blue satin coat and knee breeches, snowy white neckcloth and stockings beneath, his rather long dark hair waving back from his face, a token black mask covering his eyes. Margaret's heart had missed a beat even before she had realized that those eyes were fixed steadily on her as she sipped her lemonade and chatted animatedly to the flushed young man beside her.

Margaret had seen Brampton before at various

assemblies and had a schoolgirlish infatuation for
his handsome, romantic figure. He was older than
she, and she had very sensibly concluded that he was
beyond her touch. She would be content to worship
from afar. But now, seeing his eyes still on her, she
had flirted her fan daringly in his direction and
turned her back on him, swinging the wide skirt with
her hips as she did so.

One minute later she had felt a hand on her arm.
"Will you do me the honor of dancing the next waltz
with me, mademoiselle?" his low voice murmured
seductively into her left ear.

Margaret had pretended to consult her little
engagement booklet. "But yes, monsieur," she had
replied, with theatrical accent intact, "I see that the
next waltz is free."

He had laughed, outrageously interlaced his
fingers with hers, and led her onto the floor, leaving
the flushed young man gaping behind them.

"I hope you have been granted permission by one
of the patronesses of Almack's to waltz, my little
French angel," he had said, "or there will be scandal
for you at unmasking time."

"But yes, of course," she had replied, tossing her
head, "I have been permitted since this age ago."

He had laughed again and moved her into the
dance, holding her a little too close for strict
propriety. The tips of her breasts had touched his
blue coat on two separate occasions as he had
whirled her into a turn, doing nothing for her equil-
ibrium. She had never been this close to a man
before.

Halfway through the dance, as the movements of
the waltz had taken them close to the doors opening
onto the terrace, Brampton had murmured into her
ear, "You waltz divinely, my angel, but I think a walk

in the cool garden with you would be even more heavenly at the moment."

Everything in Margaret's training directed her to put a firm end to such an obviously improper suggestion. But Margaret had been taking a night off from her training. She had stopped close to a door, consulted her booklet, shut it with a decisive snap, and smiled dazzlingly at the earl.

"But what a coincidence, monsieur," she had lied smoothly. "I see that the next six dances are free."

He had leaned closer so that he could speak directly into her ear. "You are a little minx, my angel," he had murmured, drawing her hand through his arm and stepping out onto the terrace with her.

Other couples had been walking quietly on the terrace, the ladies fanning themselves in the cool night air. Brampton had led his prize down into the garden, where they could find a more secluded walk among the trees and flowers. He had drawn to a halt among some shady trees, leaning his back against a sturdy trunk and drawing her into the circle of his arms. Margaret had suppressed a quiver of panic.

"My little angel, let us dispense with the masks, shall we?" he had said, lifting his own away from his face so that she had gasped at the closeness of his very handsome face and blue eyes.

"No, no, monsieur," she had cried in alarm, putting a protective hand, palm outward, in front of her face, "it is vital that my identity be not revealed. We French have to beware of spies, n'est-ce pas?"

He had chuckled. "Ah, yes, Madame Guillotine is not kind to French angels. Well, let me taste these lips, little one, and see if I can guess your identity. Have they been kissed before?"

They had not. But they were soon being kissed, very thoroughly. Margaret had been thankful for his

strong arms about her. She might have buckled at
the knees otherwise. His lips had been firm and
warm on hers, his breath fanning her cheek through
the silk of the mask, and she had been headily aware
of the very masculine smell of his cologne.

He had drawn his head back finally, but not very
far. "Very nice," he had murmured, "but too much
like an angel. Come, little one, show me your fire."

And his mouth had been on hers again, open this
time, his tongue lightly tracing the line of her closed
lips. Margaret had told herself that she was going to
pull away and run back to the safety of the ballroom,
but she had found herself instead parting her lips to
allow his tongue entrance. And when its warm moistness had circled her own tongue and teased its tip
and stroked lightly over the roof of her mouth, she
had found herself without will, acting from an
instinct to be closer to him. He had molded her body
against his, her breasts pressed against his coat, the
bare skin above the low neckline of her dress tickled
by the soft folds of his neckcloth, her thighs touching
the hard muscles of his. She had heard him draw in
his breath sharply.

Brampton had loosened his hold on her while his
mouth deepened the kiss. She had not even been
shocked when she had felt his hand reaching inside
the low bodice to touch her breast. It had just been a
natural progression of what she craved. It was only
when both his hands had moved down to mold her
waist and her hips and finally to pull her hard
against him that her head had jerked back involun-
tarily. Even in her state of awakened desire, she had
been frightened by the evidence of his very obvious
arousal.

Brampton had loosened his hold immediately,

cradling her body against his, lightly holding her head against his shoulder.

"I am sorry, my angel," he had whispered softly into her ear, "I did not mean to frighten you. Are you just a little innocent after all? But a very passionate little innocent," he had commented, kissing her temple gently. "Will you remove your mask for me, little sweet?"

"No, monsieur," Margaret had replied, remembering the French accent, but her voice shaking slightly.

"Ah, but I shall discover you at unmasking time," he had teased, smiling down into her eyes, "and I shall be coming to call on you, my angel."

"Please, monsieur, I think we should go inside now," Margaret had said, and added as an afterthought, "I should like a glass of lemonade, please."

Brampton had drawn her arm gently through his again and led her back to the terrace.

"Stay here, angel," he had said, releasing her arm. "I shall bring you some lemonade without delay."

"Margaret!" a shocked voice had hissed as the earl disappeared into the ballroom. "Where have you been, my girl? Your father and I have been searching for you this half-hour past. Do you know no better, child, than to walk alone in the garden at night, with a man?"

Margaret's mother had whisked her away home without more ado, and she had not been allowed to attend any social functions for the next week.

That night had been an end and a beginning for Margaret. It had been the end of her delight in the activities of the *ton.* She had participated in a vast number of events for the rest of that Season and for the next five, and she had received three offers of marriage, one at the end of that first Season from an earnest young man who wrote a sonnet to her eyes, and two others in later years. But she had not been able to force herself either to enjoy the activities or to welcome any of the proposals. It had been the beginning of her undying and hopeless passion for the Earl of Brampton.

She had seen him with fair frequency. She had even danced with him on rare occasions, always for country dances or quadrilles, never for the waltz. And he had never shown the slightest hint of recognition or even a gleam of interest in her. Margaret had borne it all in patient silence. Only Charlotte had guessed that she had had an unhappy love experience in her past, and Charlotte thought the whole painful situation unutterably romantic.

And now, by some bizarre twist of fate, Brampton had chosen her for his bride. Margaret was in no doubt of the reason. A nobleman in his thirties, who had a reputation as a habitual womanizer, could have only one possible reason for wanting to marry a virtual stranger. He wanted children to secure his line. Like other men of his type, he would turn elsewhere for love, and she would be expected to act as if she did not know or care. Margaret suppressed a sob of despair.

But at least she would have part of him. She would share his name. She would live with him and see him daily. She would finally, after six long years, find out what it was like to be in bed with him. Margaret, even at the age of twenty-five, was still not quite sure what happened between a man and a woman in bed, but she remembered quite clearly what had started to happen to her body when he had caressed her with expert lips and tongue and hands.

Margaret shivered and sighed. And finally she closed her eyes and slept deeply.

2

RICHARD AND Margaret Adair, Earl and Countess of Brampton, sat side by side on the comfortable green velvet seat of his traveling couch. They had been wed that morning and were on their way to the earl's chief seat, Brampton Court in Hampshire, for their honeymoon. They sat now in silence, their forced and stilted conversation having flickered to an end an hour before. Margaret had her eyes closed and pretended to sleep.

Brampton looked across at her from his corner, his eyes inspecting her slowly from head to foot. She had removed her pink bonnet; it lay on the seat opposite. He looked at the brown hair, drawn severely back from her forehead and the sides of her face and coiled in heavy braids on top of her head. Not a wisp or a curl had been allowed to escape, to tease a man's imagination or make his fingers itch to explore. Her face (yes, it was definitely heart-shaped!) was composed, eyes closed, long eyelashes resting lightly against her cheeks, her lips set together.

She still wore her deep-pink velvet pelisse. It hid her figure, though he could see the regular rise and fall of her slight breasts. Her hands, clad in white kid gloves, were clasped neatly in her lap. Her feet in their white ankle boots were set side by side on the floor. He tried to feel some flicker of desire for this meek little wife of his, and felt nothing. He looked into her face again, and at the same moment, those large eyes opened and gazed blankly into his. Brampton felt that same uncomfortable jolt he had experienced on other occasions when he had unexpectedly met her eyes.

"Has the journey tired you, my dear?" he asked kindly.

"A little, my lord," she replied. "These last four weeks have been busy."

"You must call me Richard now," he said, irritated, and turned to the window to stare out at the passing countryside.

Yes, they certainly had been busy weeks, but he thanked Providence for that. He had had little time to think about the fate in store for him, little time to grasp at dishonorable schemes for getting out of his unwanted betrothal.

He had Devin Northcott to thank. His mother and Margaret's had immediately swept to the attack and taken over all the organization of the wedding. Devin, Brampton's friend since childhood, whose parents owned the estate adjoining Brampton Court, had devoted himself to filling every spare moment of his friend's time to keep his mind off his inevitable doom.

"I say, Bram," he had said on first learning of his friend's betrothal, "didn't know the wind lay in that direction. And Miss Wells? Do you have a *tendre* for her, old man?"

Brampton had snorted. "My mother's and Rosalind's choice," he had explained. "Impeccable lineage and reputation and morals and all that."

"I say, though, Bram, you are planning to turn respectable?" his friend had asked anxiously.

"Have I ever been anything but?" Brampton had raised his eyebrows and favored his friend with a haughty glare.

"Oh, say, Bram, don't come the frosty aristocrat with me," Devin had said, unperturbed. "No offense meant. Was referring to Lisa."

"I shall be quite respectable enough for my wife and my mother and my sisters—all three of them, Dev," the earl had said decisively. "What I do privately and discreetly will hurt no one."

"So Lisa stays," Devin had concluded. "Not fair to the little Miss Wells, though, Bram," he had added daringly.

Only a close friend could have got away with such open criticism of the Earl of Brampton.

"I live my own life, Dev," was the stiff reply he received.

And Devin Northcott had devoted himself to seeing that his friend enjoyed his last few weeks of freedom. They had ridden, played cards, drunk, gone to the races and to boxing mills, spent hours at Jackson's boxing saloon, and wandered from club to club at night, very often not returning home until the early hours of the morning.

Lisa had not been too perturbed by his approaching nuptials. She knew that there was no hope of his marrying her, a mere opera dancer. He was a generous and an attentive protector. She had a comfortable home, an adequate number of servants, many expensive clothes and jewels, and a generous allowance of pin money. She knew from research she had done when he had first suggested becoming her protector that he made generous settlements on his ex-mistresses. She also knew from similar research that Miss Margaret Wells was a little mouse of a woman, almost middle-aged—all of twenty-five to Lisa's twenty—and quite unlikely to be a rival in her lover's bed.

Brampton had visited her more frequently than usual in those last few weeks. He had not been sure how frequently he would be able to get away to her for the first weeks of his marriage, and Devin's comment had made him wonder whether his conscience would allow him to enjoy the illicit liaison once he was a married man. He had bedded Lisa with almost desperate passion in those weeks, allowing his body to become satiated with her practiced feminine charms. His mind had constantly made comparisons with his fiancée's body.

Gazing now out of the carriage window without seeing the passing scenery, Brampton acknowledged he felt some relief that the waiting period was finally over, that the knot was tied. Now that he knew there was definitely no way out, perhaps his mind would be less tortured. The only big ordeal ahead was the consummation of the marriage that must take place within the next few hours. Once that was over, they would be able to settle down into some sort of routine. And he would see that he spent much of his time alone. It was a while since he had visited Brampton Court; there would be plenty of estate business to keep him occupied. And his wife would have much to learn about the house and the running of the household. He would feel contented to leave her in the capable hands of Mrs. Foster, the housekeeper.

Margaret was grateful for the long silence, grateful that her husband did not feel the necessity to keep up the meaningless conversation that had occupied them for the first several miles of their journey.

She needed time to compose her mind after the frantic bustle of the last month. Her mother had taken care of all the arrangements for the wedding. She had been whisked through an endless round of visits to dressmakers, milliners, bootmakers, and the like. She had stood through hours of fittings, standing until every muscle ached as Madame Dumont pinned and measured and tucked and snipped. Margaret had thought that she had ample clothes. But it seemed that none was suitable for a bride's trousseau, especially the bride of the Earl of Brampton.

When she was not shopping or at endless fitting sessions, there were the numerous visitors to receive, flocking to congratulate her on capturing one of the greatest prizes on the matrimonial market. All seemed to think that she was incredibly fortunate; no one commented that the earl was the fortune one.

Of the earl himself, Margaret saw almost nothing. It seemed that her schedule was too full to allow of something so unimportant as meetings with her betrothed. Margaret was not sorry; she felt shy to the point of gaucheness before her very handsome fiancé.

The only person who helped Margaret keep a firm hold on sanity and apparent serenity during those weeks was Charlotte. She was ecstatic over her sister's engagement.

"Just think, Meg," she had said, clapping her hands and twirling around the drawing room, on that first day after the earl had left, "you have been insisting for the last year or more that you are just a spinster. And you have been wearing those stupid caps for the last year, though I told you and told you that you were far too pretty and had far too much character to do any such thing. And now you are to be married! And to the Earl of Brampton. He's ever so gorgeous, Meg, even though he's so old."

Margaret smiled as Charlotte paused for breath, and quietly folded her embroidery.

"You see, Meg, *he* must have realized what a diamond you are."

Margaret smiled again. "He is an older son, Lottie," she explained patiently. "He must marry soon. Do not make a grand romance out of this, my love."

"Phooey!" Charlotte commented inelegantly. "You are eminently suited, Meg. You so small and dainty and *so* pretty; and he so tall and strong and handsome."

Margaret laughed. "You are looking through the eyes of a fond sister," she said. "I fear not many people would agree with you."

"Well, perhaps he is not *that* strong or *that* handsome," Charlotte agreed mischievously.

"You know what I meant," Margaret replied, smiling affectionately at her sister.

Charlotte was to be bridesmaid at the wedding and delighted in every moment of the fittings and the shopping sprees. She had not yet made her come-out, and to her, all the activity was magical. Through a complicated set of negotiations that involved mainly the mothers of the bride and groom, it was agreed that Charlotte would live with her sister and brother-in-law for the Season, after they returned from Hampshire, and that Margaret would undertake to chaperone her come-out. Mr. Wells was relieved to have the chance to return to his own estate after the unexpected expense of Margaret's wedding. Both sisters were delighted by the arrangement.

Margaret wished that they were already back in London. Surely life would be easier there, where there would be numerous activities to occupy their time and furnish them with topics of conversation, and where Charlotte's vivacious personality would fill in any awkward silences.

Margaret was dreading the next week. What would they do to occupy the days? Would Richard take it upon himself to entertain her? She wished for and dreaded such intimacy. How would she converse with him without appearing dull or stupid or silly? Would he go about his own business and leave her to her own devices?

And, of course, the biggest ordeal of all was the night ahead. Would he kiss and caress her as he had so long ago in the Hetheringtons' garden? Her breathing quickened at the thought and she made an effort to control it. She opened her eyes for a moment and found herself looking straight into her husband's eyes. She felt dazed with shock until he asked her if she was tired.

A minute later, as Brampton turned away to the window, Margaret bit her lip. She had seen the flash of annoyance in his eyes as she had called him "my lord." She must accustom herself to calling him Richard, though it seemed too great a familiarity. Goodness, this man was now her husband!

What was he going to think of her tonight? Margaret knew that he was experienced with women. His caresses had told her that six years before. But she had also heard of his many affairs and knew that he kept mistresses. Did he have one now? A sharp stab of pain and jealousy hit her. And she really did not know how to please him. She did not even know what came after the stage of love-making they had reached in the garden, though she knew that it had something to do with the bulge of desire she had felt when he had pulled her against him. She must just learn. She drew some comfort from his remembered words. He had called her a "very passionate little innocent." Would it be enough?

Margaret sighed inaudibly, opened her eyes, and turned to gaze sightlessly out of the window on her side of the carriage. No point in teasing herself over something that she could not control.

Margaret sat at the dresser while Kitty brushed her long wavy hair until it shone.

"Braid it, please, Kitty," she instructed.

"Oh, miss—I mean, my lady, it looks so lovely this way. Leave it just for tonight."

"No. The braids, Kitty," Margaret answered firmly. She did not understand herself. She recognized that she looked feminine, almost attractive, with her hair down. And she knew that the braids made her look prim—Charlotte had told her so often enough. She wanted to attract her husband's admiration, but she could not bring herself to cast out deliberate lures. For the same reason, she had chosen a high-necked, long-sleeved nightgown that swept the floor. The only concession she had made to Charlotte's loud protests was the liberal amount of lace that trimmed it. Kitty had unpacked it earlier with the rest of her trousseau that had come in a baggage coach, with Kitty and Stevens.

Kitty pursed her lips when Margaret rose from the stool. She obviously did not approve either of the nightgown or of the heavy braid draped over each shoulder as suitable for her mistress's wedding night.

"Shall I wait, my lady?" she asked doubtfully as Margaret climbed into the huge four-poster bed with its heavy gold brocade hangings.

"No, Kitty, you may leave." Margaret suppressed a panic-stricken urge to make some excuse to keep her maid with her. "And you may leave the candle burning."

Kitty gave her an anxious glance, curtsied, and withdrew.

Margaret slid down on the pillows and forced herself to wait calmly. How long would he be? She had left him downstairs in the drawing room. He had some business to attend to, he had explained, before he retired. How should she behave? Should she respond as she had before? Would he think her wanton? Would he be disgusted to find that he had a wife who would welcome his lovemaking eagerly and with passion? Should she behave with quiet decorum as she would be expected by her mother to behave on such an occasion?

Her thoughts whirled on until she heard the door that led from his bedroom into the adjoining dressing room open. Her heart hammered until she was afraid that she would not be able to breathe. Almost immediately, there was a soft tap on the door that led from her room into the dressing room. Brampton did not wait for an answer; he entered his wife's bedroom.

He was wearing a dark-red, silk dressing gown. The snowy white neckline of his nightshirt showed beneath. Margaret fixed her eyes on his face, afraid that she would lose her courage otherwise. He walked across to the bed and looked down into her large, calm eyes. He sat down on the edge of the bed.

"You have had an exhausting day, my dear," he said quietly, searching her face for some expression that would give sign of her feelings. Did she have none? "Perhaps you would prefer that I should bid you good night?"

"I am not overtired, my lord—Richard," she said softly. Had she really said that? How brazen it sounded once the words were out of her mouth. But she could not bear to put this off, to have to go through the same torture again tomorrow night.

Brampton looked into her face for a few seconds more, then leaned over to the side table and blew out the candle. Margaret felt his weight lifting from the bed, presumably while he removed his dressing gown, and then he was in the bed beside her. She put her arms at her sides, moist palms flat on the bedsheet, and forced herself to relax.

He leaned across her and with an incredibly deft movement of his hands lifted her nightgown to her waist. Margaret barely suppressed a gasp of humiliation. He moved across her and lowered his weight onto her body so that she was crushed between him and the mattress. His hands went beneath her and tilted her closer to him at the same time as his knees came between her thighs and forced her legs wide apart. Before Margaret could react to the panic that was threatening to overwhelm her, she felt an unfamiliar hardness press against her.

Brampton paused in his entry when he felt the resistance of her virginity. He raised his head and looked briefly into her eyes, which were like shadowed pools in the darkness of the room. Damn! He had never entered a virgin before. Was he about to hurt her badly? He pushed himself carefully the rest of the way in. She did not flinch.

Margaret dug her fingers, clawlike, into the mattress and concentrated on her breathing. Was this it? Was it over now?

Brampton moved his hands to her shoulders, pinning them to the bed, and began to thrust with deep, firm strokes, working himself to a climax as quickly as he could. When he was finished, he relaxed against her for a few seconds, then lifted his head once more to look down at her. She still had her eyes open, staring up at him. Had he hurt her? It must be dreadful to be a woman in her situation. As he disengaged himself gently from her body, he raised one hand and brushed the knuckles softly over her cheek. He felt the stirring of some emotion—tenderness? No, definitely not that. Compassion?

"Did I hurt you, my dear?" he murmured.

"No, Richard." The voice was higher-pitched than usual, but quite firm.

He lifted himself away from her, swung off the bed, and put his dressing gown back on over his nightshirt. He paused before leaving the room.

"Sleep well, my dear," he said. "You need rest."

And he was gone.

Back in his own room, Brampton sank into a brocaded chair close to the blazing fire that a footman had built up a short while before, and blew out his breath through puffed cheeks.

That was over!

And really it had not been so bad. He had been horribly afraid that he might have to cope with maidenly tears or hysterics. He had to admit that his wife had class. She must have been terrified near out of her wits, and he knew he must have hurt her. But she had neither flinched nor murmured. Her body beneath his had felt strange, although, out of respect for her feelings, he had not explored it. He was used to choosing for himself women with more hills and curves. But her slight little figure had not felt totally unpleasant.

Having to visit her bed regularly until she was with child might not be quite as distasteful as he had anticipated.

Margaret lay in shock. It had been horrible, horrible! She had known that he did not love her, that he had married her only because he needed a wife and a mother for his children. But she was still aghast at the discovery of just how indifferent to her he was.

He had been totally uninterested in her body or her feelings. There had been no attempt to prepare her, to get her ready either physically or emotionally for his invasion. And in all her imaginings, she had never dreamed of such a deep and ruthless occupation of her body.

He had not made the slightest attempt to find out what she had to offer him. He had used her—yes, quite dispassionately used her, for only one purpose: to sow his seed in her womb.

Oh, she hated him, hated him!

Margaret slammed her face into one pillow and pulled another over her head to stifle the deep and painful sobs that racked her body for many minutes before she finally fell into an exhausted and unhappy sleep.

3

THE EARL of Brampton lay staring at the hangings above the bed. His body was totally relaxed and sated after three consecutive sessions of lovemaking. Lisa's head lay in the crook of his arm, her blond hair spread in disarray over his arm and chest. One full white breast lay against his side. One of her knees had been pushed beneath his. She was asleep, breathing deeply and evenly.

He was still not satisfied, though he knew he would not have the energy to take her again that afternoon. It was three weeks since his return to London, five weeks since his wedding. He could not explain to himself why he had not visited her before now. He had wanted to, but had kept putting it off. He had persuaded himself that he was too busy with the come-out ball he and his wife had given in honor of Charlotte the night before. In truth, though, he admitted now, his own part in those preparations had been negligible. His wife had taken charge of the invitations, the food and flower arrangements, the cleaning and decoration of the ballroom, and all the other trivia, with a quiet and suprisingly efficient energy. In the last three weeks he had really done little more than visit all his old haunts with Devin Northcott.

He had finally persuaded himself that he was free

and eager this afternoon. Lisa had welcomed him with flattering enthusiasm.

"Ah, Richard, you naughty, naughty man," she had said, pouting her full lips and throwing her arms around his neck. "I was sure that you had forgotten all about your Lisa. Maybe your wife is prettier and more charming than I. Maybe she satisfies you more than your Lisa." She had fluttered her eyelashes at him and run a finger down each side of his carefully folded neckcloth.

She had so obviously been fishing for compliments, Brampton had found himself unexpectedly annoyed.

"Lisa, we will get one thing straight," he had said sternly, grasping her wrists firmly and removing her hands from his chest. "We will leave my wife out of all conversations. Is that understood?"

For once, she had looked unsure of herself. "Of course, Richard," she had said.

But after he had sunk into a chair in her small drawing room, she had come to sit on the arm and had chatted easily while smoothing his hair back from his brow and rubbing her finger tantalizingly across the nape of his neck. At last, she had moved to his lap and carefully untied his neckcloth and unbuttoned his shirt. Aroused, Brampton had carried her to the bedroom.

What had been wrong with the afternoon? he wondered. Lisa had made every effort to please him, using all the arts and wiles he and previous lovers had taught her. And he had been pleased—pleased to throw off the restraint he practiced in his wife's bed. He had taken her with fierce, unleashed lust.

He did not feel that he was doing anything particularly wrong, visiting a mistress while his wife sat at home receiving visitors after the ball of the night before. The practice of keeping mistresses was well accepted in his circles. In fact, it could be argued that such arrangements protected the tender sensibilities of the wives. They gave their husbands an outlet for their wilder passions. Brampton tried to imagine using his wife as he had used Lisa this afternoon. He tried to feel amusement at the thought, but felt only guilt.

Guilt? Yes, he admitted that he had no right to make her into a figure of fun, even in his imagination. He certainly did not love her, he did not even find her attractive, but she had won his grudging respect in the short duration of their marriage.

He had lengthened their stay at Brampton Court from one week to two, finding himself oddly contented in the country. He had not spent much time with his wife, but more than he had planned. He had discovered to his surprise that she could ride and had mounted her on a quiet mare from his stables. She had not told him that riding was one of her favorite pastimes, that at home in Leicestershire she had often taken out her father's horse, riding him demurely except on those occasions when she could get away without an attendant; then she would wait until she was out of sight of the house, hitch her skirts inelegantly, swing one leg over the saddle so that she was riding astride, and gallop until her cheeks and eyes glowed.

Brampton had patiently reduced the speed of his own mount to suit the sedate pace of hers and had ridden with her all over the estate. He remembered one afternoon in particular. He had taken her to visit some of his tenants, poor cottagers who were wide-eyed and agog at meeting the new countess.

They were sitting inside one of the cottages while the woman of the house, flustered, pressed cider and cakes on them. A small toddler, newly come inside from a game of building mud pies, waddled up to Margaret and put a dirty hand on her skirt. Margaret smiled down at the child.

"Tommy, come away," hissed his almost frantic mother, making a dive for him.

"Oh, please, Mrs. Hope, don't mind him," Margaret had smiled. "He is a darling." And she had touched the child's soft blond curls.

"Oh, my lady, he'll soil your lovely habit," Mrs. Hope had protested.

"I have other clothes," Margaret had replied, "and this will wash. I so rarely have the chance to cuddle a child." And she had lifted Tommy to her lap and laughed as he reached for and pulled the earrings that dangled within his reach.

"Ouch!" she had protested, and she imprisoned his fingers in hers and eased them away from the earring. And she had glanced across at her husband, a laugh in her eyes. It was only then that Brampton had realized that he had been staring, mesmerized.

He had discovered during the rest of that two-week honeymoon that his earlier opinion that she was dull was not correct. She was quiet. She seemed to have little sense of humor. And she made no attempt to use her femininity. But she had good sense and a bright mind. Her conversation was never silly or tedious. If she had nothing to say, she simply said nothing.

And for some very curious reason that he could not fathom, Brampton had come to look forward to the few minutes he spent in her bed each night. He had missed the ritual when, a few days before their return to London, she had had to inform him, blushing painfully (almost the only open sign of emotion he had ever seen in her) that he should not visit her

room for the following five nights. She had even forgotten herself enough on that occasion to call him
"my lord" again. He had not drawn her attention to
the lapse.

Lisa had turned her head into his shoulder and was
nuzzling his neck, biting the skin lightly with her
small teeth. She purred like a cat.

"Richard, my love, I swear you are a wild animal
today," she sighed contentedly. "I shall be covered
with bruises tomorrow."

"My apologies," Brampton replied coldly. He
pulled his arm from beneath her body and rolled off
the bed. He stood up and began to dress, wrinkling
his nose distastefully at the smell of her perfume on
his skin.

"I shall not be visiting here again, Lisa," he heard
himself saying. He had certainly not planned to say
any such thing.

"What!" she exclaimed from the bed behind him.

"I am a married man," he said. "I owe my wife
better than this. The house is yours, of course, and
all its furnishings. I shall arrange with my man of
business to make a settlement on you. I am sure you
will find it satisfactory."

He dressed quickly and left the house while she
was still crying and pleading. He did not feel very
proud of himself.

Charlotte sat down beside Margaret on the
drawing-room sofa. She stretched her legs out
straight ahead of her and rested her head against a
soft cushion.

"Oh, Meg," she sighed, "this is so exciting and so
tiring, is it not?"

"Are you pleased, love?" her sister replied, smiling
gently and glancing up from her embroidery. "You

certainly seem to have made an impression. All the young men were clamoring to dance with you last night. I do believe Richard was almost disappointed. He was fully prepared to lead you out himself if there was any danger of your being a wallflower."

"And three calls from admirers this afternoon!" Charlotte exclaimed with an artless lack of modesty. "And all these flowers, Meg." She looked around at the posies and bouquets that had been delivered that morning, all from young men she had met the night before.

Margaret smiled again. "I am so happy for you, Lottie. I can remember how exciting my own first Season was."

Charlotte must have detected the wistful note in her sister's voice. She immediately sat up straight and regarded her sister intently.

"Meg, I wish you would not sit there so calmly at your needlework and wearing that oh-so-stupid cap, just like a—a—"

"Matron?"

"Yes, like a matron. You are a bride, Meg," her sister cried passionately. "What is the matter? You and Lord Brampton behave as if you have been wed for years. And I was sure that you would suit admirably. You aren't happy, are you, Meg?"

Margaret winced. Her sister had all the bluntness of extreme youth. "Of course I am happy," she said soothingly. "Why ever would I not be?"

"No, you aren't. You do not even try to make yourself pleasing to my brother-in-law," Charlotte accused. "I mean, really pleasing. Has he ever seen you without your hair braided? Has he ever seen you laugh? Oh, Meg, I love you dearly, but why must you hide your real self? I know you are the loveliest, sweetest, warmest person in the world." And she impulsively moved along the sofa and hugged her sister.

"It is no good, Lottie," Margaret said mildly. "You cannot turn this marriage into the grand romance. It is a marriage like most of the other marriages of people of our kind—no worse."

"Ah, but, Meg, you did love once, did you not?" Charlotte asked.

"Yes, once—when I was very young and very foolish."

"I do not believe you were ever foolish, Meg," her sister said, gazing at Margaret loyally. She hesitated a moment, then asked, "Do you love him still, Meg?"

Margaret's fingers paused over her work. "Yes," she said.

"Who was he, Meg?"

There was a longer pause. "Richard," Margaret said.

"What?"

Margaret resumed her sewing. "It was Richard I fell in love with six years ago," she said.

"But I do not understand," Charlotte said. "Did he not love you? But why has he married you now?"

"He did not know who I was," Margaret said with a sigh. "It was really all very foolish. And I do not know why I am telling you all this after so long." She proceeded to give Charlotte an edited version of what had happened that night at the Hetheringtons' masquerade ball.

"I think it was a great foolishness not to take off your mask when he begged you to," Charlotte commented. "Then he would have known you and he would have called on you as he said he would, and you would have been married years ago and it would have been a lovely marriage, full of love and romance."

"Perhaps," Margaret smiled sadly.

"But this is all foolishness," Charlotte exclaimed, leaping to her feet and pacing restlessly around the room. "You must tell him the truth."

Margaret laughed. "Do you suggest, my love, that I say to him at the breakfast table, 'Oh, by the by, Richard, do you remember the little girl dressed as Marie Antoinette at a masquerade party six years ago? The one you kissed in the garden and called your angel? That was me!' He would think I had taken leave of my senses, Lottie. He would not even recollect the incident."

"Phooey! I do see your point about not being able to broach the topic, though, Meg." Charlotte's brow puckered with concentration. "I am going to return to my room and think. We need a plan! I think it might be necessary to resurrect Marie Antoinette." And she skipped lightly from the room, closing the door behind her.

Margaret let her hands relax in her lap, her embroidery forgotten. Why had she told Charlotte? She was not sure. Some compulsion, perhaps, to share her pain. Or was it that Charlotte's come-out had reminded her so strongly of her own?

Despite what Charlotte had said, Margaret was not actively unhappy. After that first traumatic night of her honeymoon, she had gradually picked up the pieces of her dignity and retreated behind her usual facade of quiet serenity. Her husband was neither cruel not neglectful. For the two weeks of their honeymoon, she had spent much time alone or with the housekeeper. But she had also spent more time with her husband than she had expected. He had taken pains to show her his estate and to introduce her to all his tenants, as well as to his neighbors, the Northcotts.

Margaret had drawn a secret pleasure from the fact that he always introduced her not just as the countess, but as "my wife, the Countess of Brampton."

She found it very hard to adjust to her bitter disappointment over their sexual relations. Each night was an exact repetition of the first, except that there was never again the pain and that he never again made the almost tender gesture of touching her cheek. He never kissed her, never talked to her, never caressed any part of her, never lingered longer than one minute after his business had been completed.

She had to convince herself that most wives probably had little more than she had. Her mother, in fact, in a speech of advice on her wedding morning, had warned that marriage would be very pleasant if she were a dutiful wife. She must learn, in exchange for all the contentment, to endure her husband's "attentions" at night "for a few minutes only, my love." Margaret admitted that, had she behaved with propriety at the masquerade ball, she would not even know that physical contant with a man might be exciting.

She trained herself to enjoy those few minutes for what they were worth. For that short span of time each night, her husband was all hers. Sometimes, if he was later than usual coming to her room, she would find her body aroused from just thinking of what was about to happen. And then his arrival was an agony. She had to keep every physical sign of her arousal strictly concealed and she had to endure the terrible frustration of having neither the time nor the freedom to reach for the unknown something that the weight of his body and his brief lovemaking made her own body ache for.

No, Margaret was not unhappy. She resumed her embroidery.

Charlotte perfected the plan the next day while driving in Hyde Park with Devin Northcott. She had puzzled over it so much after leaving Margaret in the drawing room that she had given herself a headache. So quiet was she at dinner that night, in fact, that Brampton commented on it.

"Are you feeling quite well, Charlotte?" he asked with concern.

"What? Oh, yes, my lord," she answered. "Just a little tired, maybe, after last night's ball."

"And did you enjoy yourself?" he asked. "You most certainly did not lack for partners."

"Oh, it was ever so much fun, my lord," Charlotte began, her natural enthusiasm for life beginning to bubble again. But she was immediately struck by a thought that had her once more silent and dreaming.

Should she suggest that Lord Brampton give a masquerade ball in his home so that Meg could appear mysteriously as Marie Antoinette and bowl him off his feet? No, it would not work. How would anyone explain away the disappearance of the hostess?

"Northcott informs me that he is to take you driving tomorrow," Brampton commented. Having broken off his relationship with Lisa just that afternoon, he felt somewhat ill-at-ease with his wife, and was anxious to keep Charlotte talking. Usually she chattered on without any encouragement.

"Yes, my lord. He has a new high-perch phaeton, and I have a new bonnet," Charlotte explained, as if these facts justified the situation entirely. "And Meg says that it would be quite unexceptionable for me to accept the invitation."

"Oh, quite," replied Brampton, glancing down the table to his wife. She was smiling affectionately at her sister, her usual quiet, calm self.

Charlotte's thoughts were on the wing again. Could she ask Mr. Northcott to give a masquerade party? No, he occupied only bachelor rooms. Anyway, she was still a little shy of him because he was so old (somewhere in the region of Lord Brampton's age, she guessed) and was so much the perfect gentleman of fashion. She had found it easy to converse with him during the two dances they had shared the night before and during his visit that afternoon, but she did not think she yet had the courage to ask so great a favor of him.

The London weather cooperated for the afternoon drive. It was a perfect spring day. Charlotte was able to wear her new apple-green muslin dress and the matching parasol with brown fringes. Her brown bonnet was trimmed with green, yellow, and straw-colored leaves and flowers that complemented her auburn hair. Devin Northcott thought she made a perfect picture in his new phaeton and told her so.

Charlotte admired his appearance no less. He wore biscuit-colored buckskins and white-tasseled Hessian boots that shone so brightly she felt she would be able to see her face in them if she leaned forward. His dark-green coat had the perfect cut that only the renowned Weston could have tailored; his snowy-white neckcloth had been arranged in complicated folds, though Charlotte could not put a name to the creation. Was it a waterfall? A mathematical? He wore a dark beaver on his fair hair. Devin Northcott was not a tall man, and he had a slight figure, but Charlotte concluded that she liked his air of kindly gentility.

They arrived at Hyde Park at the fashionable hour

of five o'clock. It seemed that half the *haut monde* were there, most people wheeling around slowly in carriages of various descriptions, some on horseback, a few on foot. Everyone was there to see and to be seen, to nod at acquaintances, to cut enemies, to exchange the latest *on-dits* with friends.

Charlotte enjoyed herself thoroughly. She found herself admired and ogled by several young bucks, some of whom she had met at the Brampton ball two nights before. She was soon twirling her parasol with confident gaiety.

When they were not exchanging pleasantries with various acquaintances, Northcott entertained Charlotte with an enumeration of all the pleasurable activities she could experience now that she was "out." She listened with one ear while she enjoyed the sights and sensations of the park.

"And you will have to visit Vauxhall Gardens," he was saying. "Beautiful outdoor gardens lit by lanterns: music, food, masked guests . . ."

The plan was born in Charlotte's brain full-grown. She reacted with lightning promptness.

"Oh, Mr. Northcott," she sighed, giving the parasol a light twirl, "it sounds so *heavenly*. Alas, I do not think it is the type of entertainment to appeal to Meg and my brother-in-law. They are really dears, you know, but somewhat—"

"Stuffy?" supplied the obliging Mr. Northcott.

"I hate to appear disloyal," Charlotte breathed, lowering her lashes.

"Say no more, Miss Wells," said the gallant Devin. "You would do me a great honor if you would join a party to Vauxhall that I plan to make up. I have some influence with your brother-in-law and will guarantee that he and your sister will be of the party."

"Oh, would you!" Charlotte gushed, hands clasped together over the handle of her parasol, eyes wide and worshipful. "That would be divine."

Devin returned Charlotte to Brampton's house and drove away feeling like public benefactor number one, and convinced that the little chit was not really as silly as the bulk of the new crop of debutantes. Quite a fetching little thing, in fact!

"Meg, Meg." Charlotte took the stairs, with shocking inelegance, two at a time. She burst into the drawing room to find her sister reclining on a chaise longue, reading a book.

"Lottie, my love, what is it?" Margaret asked, laying aside the book and regarding her sister with some alarm. "Did Mr. Northcott upset the phaeton?"

"Oh, no, no, nothing like that," Charlotte answered impatiently, tossing parasol, bonnet, and gloves onto the chair closest to the door, "but Mr. Northcott is to see that we all go to Vauxhall one night and you and Lord Brampton are to go too, but you are not to go, but you are to go as Marie Antoinette, but Lord Brampton will think you are not there, but you will be there, of course, although he won't know it, and then he will fall in love with you, though he won't know it's you—and you will live happily ever after!" She finished with a flourish and beamed.

Margaret stared and then laughed. "Lottie, my love, I lost you after 'Vauxhall,' " she said.

Charlotte sank down onto the sofa with a resigned sigh. "I shall explain again," she said. "Oh, Meg, please, could we ring for tea?"

Margaret got to her feet and obligingly rang the bell.

Charlotte began again. "Mr. Northcott has promised to make up a party to go to Vauxhall

Gardens one night," she said. "He told me that almost everyone goes there wearing masks. The thing is, Meg, that you and Lord Brampton must accept the invitation, but at the last moment you must stay behind—you must have the headache, I think. Lord Brampton must go, of course, to accompany me.

"When we are gone, you will dress as Marie Antoinette again, with a mask; then you must follow us to the gardens and made sure that Lord Brampton sees you. Then he will fall in love with you and you can reveal your real identity. It can't fail, Meg."

"It is quite the most absurd plan I ever heard in my life," said Margaret.

"Name one thing wrong with it."

"I can name several," she said. "For one thing, I am no longer a girl to play games. Second, I do not still have the costume of Marie Antoinette. Third, how would I get to Vauxhall alone at night? Fourth, Richard would probably not give me a second glance even if I were dressed as before. Fifth, if he *did* pursue me, he would recognize me immediately. Sixth, it is wrong to play such tricks on my husband. And seventh, it couldn't possibly work—could it, Lottie?"

"Of course it would work," Charlotte replied, quite undaunted by the list of objections. And she crossed to the chaise longue, sat beside her sister, poured the tea, which had arrived a few minutes before, and proceeded to hammer out an ironproof battle plan.

"Oh, Lottie, do you *really* think it might work?" Margaret asked anxiously fifteen minutes later, her voice almost pleading. "I really do not believe I *could*."

"Phooey!" her sister replied.

4

THE DATE FOR the visit to Vauxhall Gardens was set for three weeks in the future. Devin Northcott had wanted to make it sooner, but the ladies of the Brampton household were strangely full of excuses. There could be no doubt, though, that they wanted very much to go. The party was to be made up of Devin, the Earl and Countess of Brampton, Charlotte, and Sir Henry and Lady Lucy Wood, the latter being Brampton's youngest sister.

Margaret and Charlotte were extremely busy with all the activities of the latter's come-out. The days were filled with shopping expeditions, visits, rides in the park; almost every evening had its activity—the theater, the opera, musicales, balls, dinners. Now they found that preparations for the evening at Vauxhall had to be fitted into the busy schedule.

Charlotte was easily accommodated. Madame Dumont undertook the not-too-demanding task of making her a domino and a frilled mask, both of emerald-green satin. Margaret visited the costumier from whom she had hired her costume six years before, not at all hopeful that the Marie Antoinette outfit would still be available. Even so, she was disappointed to discover that she was right.

She was ready to abandon the scheme there and then. Charlotte, however, was more resourceful. She found out from Kitty the name of the dressmaker who had her workrooms in a street of London not quite as fashionable as Bond Street. She dragged her sister there the following afternoon and together Margaret and Miss Thomas sketched a dress that closely resembled the one Margaret had worn before. She chose a similar fabric, too—a heavy silver brocaded silk. She also agreed to Miss Thomas' suggestion that the full skirt be decorated with seed pearls to give it extra weight and sparkle.

A mask was also agreed upon—silver silk, as before, to cover her forehead, cheeks, and most of her nose.

Then the sisters had to visit a wigmaker's, not so easy to find now that wigs for everyday use had fallen out of fashion. Margaret was fitted for an elaborate powdered creation, typical of those worn by the ladies of a couple of decades before, high on the crown, one ringlet to drape over a shoulder.

To complete the outfit, they shopped for bright wine-colored slippers to match the fan that Margaret had used on the previous occasion and that she still possessed. She also bought some lip rouge, feeling very daring. She had never owned cosmetics before, but felt that the silver-and-white garments would need a little color. The lips, fan, and shoes would add just the necessary touch.

Kitty had to be taken into Margaret's confidence. She was going to need help on the night of Vauxhall, and Charlotte would not be available. She had expected Kitty to be downright disapproving. She had even been a little afraid that Kitty would rush off to tell Richard. She reckoned without the fierce love of her maid, who had appeared tight-lipped and disapproving for the last couple of years because she felt that her mistress was deliberately hiding her charm and beauty. Her own husband, for example, had never seen her hair except in its tight braids. And Margaret's hair, under the loving strokes of Kitty's brush hand, was her crowning glory—thick, shining, wavy, and waist-length.

Kitty was as excited as Charlotte by the plan. But she did veto one of the details. She was horrified by the idea of having her mistress hire a hackney cab to take her to Vauxhall and bring her back again.

"No, my lady," she had said, her lips setting in a thin line of obstinacy, "it just won't do. I'm not going to have my lady jaunting all over London alone at night, so don't you think it."

But it was Kitty who finally hit on the solution. She was "stepping out" with Jem, one of his lordship's grooms. She had a private conference with him and he declared that he would have no problem in taking out his lordship's plain town carriage on that night and driving her ladyship to Vauxhall himself. He added another suggestion of his own. He would wear a plain domino and mask so that he could accompany the countess into the gardens and make sure that no harm came to her before she met the earl.

Both Kitty and Jem were told that the whole escapade was to be a prank to see if the Earl of Brampton would recognize his wife in costume. Kitty, though, who remembered another Marie Antoinette costume years before and who knew that her mistress and his lordship did not have as close and loving a relationship as Kitty would have liked, put two and two together and came up with four. She kept her own counsel, though. She said nothing either to the countess or to Jem.

Brampton looked forward with some amusement

to the party to Vauxhall. He had been observing with curiosity his friend coming more and more under the spell of Charlotte's charms.

"If you do not have a care," he warned his friend one morning at White's while both were supposedly perusing the daily newspaper, "you are going to be the next one to be leg-shackled, Dev!"

"The devil!" his companion replied. "You mean Miss Wells? No, no, Bram, just being kind to the chit. Her being Lady Bram's sister, y'know."

"It seems to me she does not need kindness," Brampton replied dryly. "The young bucks are lined up three deep for half a block waiting to pay their respects."

"No good, Bram," Devin protested. "Such a young, innocent little thing. Needs someone older and steadier to protect her from all those sparks."

Brampton laughed. "You are doing it too brown, Dev. You steady? You the protector of innocence? I tell you, Dev, it's love pure and simple." And he returned, smiling, to his newspaper while his companion sputtered his protests.

Brampton had no particular objection to spending a whole evening in his wife's company. Ever since his breakup with Lisa, he had been determined at least to try to make something of his marriage. He could not imagine that there would ever be any deep feeling between them. She was not lively enough to excite any great interest in him; she obviously was not a woman who could feel deep passion and she would certainly not welcome any demonstration of feeling from him beyond a mild affection.

But that mild affection he was prepared to give. She had really interfered hardly at all with his life. He had feared that he would never again feel at home in his own house after his wedding. Yet he found that he felt more so. His wife never invaded his own sanctuary, the library. She did not litter the house with her possessions. She did not fill the house with noise and bustle. But he did notice that his favorite foods were served far more frequently than they used to be, that his brandy decanter and the snuff box in the library were always well supplied, that his comings and goings were never questioned.

Brampton felt rather ashamed, in fact, of ever having thought of his wife as an antidote. She was not a beauty and her face lacked vivacity, but it was a sweet face and she had eyes that could have transformed her into a beauty if they would only sparkle.

He sometimes wished that she did have some vitality. He would have liked to see her smile more often. He would have liked to touch her with his hands, to explore the quiet, disciplined little body, to touch that sweet mouth with his own. But he never overindulged in such thoughts. He did not wish to arouse loathing or disgust in his wife. And he was quite convinced that she would be disgusted by such physical advances. So he made an effort in her bed to cover her body with his without invading her privacy more than was necessary, and to occupy her body for as short a time as possible.

Brampton was, in fact, working had at his marriage.

Sir Henry, Lady Lucy, and Devin Northcott had been invited to dine with the earl and his countess on the night of the outing to Vauxhall.

Margaret made sure that she was late entering the drawing room before dinner. The guests had all arrived. She noticed only, in her mood of tense excitement, that Richard was looking more than usually magnificent in dark gold-colored knee breeches and coat, a chocolate-brown waistcoat making his shirt and intricately styled neckcloth seem startlingly white in contrast.

When he raised a hand to signal a footman to bring her a drink, Margaret was careful to raise heavy-lidded eyes to him.

"Nothing, thank you, Richard," she said.

His eyes searched her face. "Are you all right, my dear?" he asked quietly.

"Yes, of course, Richard," she replied brightly and a little too quickly.

A few minutes later, when Chalmer announced dinner, Brampton offered his arm to his wife, instead of to his sister, as strict good manners would have dictated, and escorted her into the dining room.

Margaret was listless throughout the meal. She said little, toyed with the food on her plate, drank no wine, and put two fingertips to her temples a few times, removing them hastily and smiling vaguely when she caught Richard's eye.

After the meal, the men rejoined the ladies in the drawing room without much delay, as they wished to make a prompt departure for Vauxhall. Brampton immediately seated himself beside his wife on a love seat.

"My dear, you are unwell?" he asked, concerned.

"Just a little headache, Richard," she replied, smiling wanly. "I shall be fine."

"We must stay at home, then," he said. "You must have some laudanum, my dear, and retire to bed."

"Oh, no, Richard," Margaret protested, "it is really nothing. I cannot spoil the entertainment for everyone."

"Your health is of more importance than other people's entertainment," her husband said deciisively. "We shall remain at home. There is still a party of four."

"But, Richard," Margaret pleaded, "I cannot like Charlotte going out without us to chaperon her. I know that Lucy will take care of her, but I really feel the responsibility left with me by Mama and Papa."

"She will be quite safe, my dear. You must think of yourself once in a while, you know."

"Richard," she said, looking him full in the face with soulful eyes, "would you do me a great favor and accompany them?" And she very daringly placed her hand on his, until her thumping heart and quickened breathing forced her to remove it.

Brampton hesitated. He could not remember any other occasion when his wife had asked him to do something for her. He considered with dismay the prospect of an evening spent alone with two couples. He would feel like a wallflower par excellence.

"Very well, my dear," he said, "but only on condition that you go to your bed immediately. I shall send Kitty up to you."

"Thank you, Richard," she said, and slipped quietly from the room, leaving Brampton to make her excuses. He sat on for a few moments after she had left, worrying about her. He had never known her unwell. She could not be pregnant. He had been denied her bed again for five nights less than two weeks before. Perhaps she was working too hard to make Charlotte's Season a success.

Margaret forced herself to lie in bed for ten minutes after she had heard the party leave for Vauxhall. She was glad that she had taken the precaution of going to bed. Richard himself had brought her the laudanum and a warm drink of milk.

She had claimed that the milk was too hot to drink but had promised to take the medicine as soon as the drink had cooled.

He had sat on the edge of the bed, suffocating her with his aura of masculinity.

"My poor dear," he had said. "You have been so looking forward to this evening, have you not?"

"Yes, Richard," she had replied, "but it is Charlotte I am really concerned about. She has been so excited."

"I shall take you there another evening," he had said, smiling gently into her eyes, unaware of the somersaults his expression was causing her stomach and heart to perform.

"That would be nice, Richard," she had replied.

And then she could have sworn that her stomach and heart changed places when he leaned slightly toward her. She was certain that he was about to kiss her. But he merely put back a strand of hair that had worked loose from the braids that were still coiled around the back of her head; then he laid gentle fingertips against one of her cheeks for a moment.

"Good night, my dear," he had said. "Sleep well and have no fears for Charlotte. I shall be as good a chaperon as you could wish."

Kitty finally arrived in the bedroom and Margaret leapt out of the bed, her body and mind all aflutter at the thought of what lay ahead that night. Kitty was carrying the silver gown over her arm. The accessories were quickly dragged from boxes in the bedroom closets.

Half an hour later, Margaret was ready to leave. She surveyed herself one more time in the full-length mirror. As far as she could remember, she looked almost exactly as she had looked on that night long ago when she had first danced with, and first kissed,

Richard. The gown was a trifle more gorgeous, and she had a suspicion that the neckline was a trifle lower, but it had the same design—a tight bodice and short, puffed sleeves, a very full skirt, wide on the hips. The wig looked the same, adding height and elegance to Margaret's slight, slim form. Her coiled braids would not fit beneath the wig; her long brown hair was pinned loosely beneath it. Her mask was tied securely to the back of her head, beneath the wig. It covered most of her face, so that she was almost convinced that she would be unrecognizable.

Almost convinced, but not quite! For the last three weeks, Margaret had been plagued by doubts as strong as her excitement. She was largely convinced that Richard would pay her no attention at all. Why should he? He had had—and probably still had—dozens of lovely women. Why should he remember one girl whom he had kissed and fondled for a half-hour six years before? She would be disappointed to be totally ignored.

But what really terrified her was that Richard might take notice. What if he tried to talk to her? Would he not immediately recognize her? And what would she say if he did? She had had three weeks in which to make up a story that would cover such an eventuality, but she had still not thought of one. She just hoped that, if the crisis occurred, she would receive inspiration on the spot.

Kitty, who had left to confer with Jem, poked her head around the door again and announced in a stage whisper, "The carriage is ready, my lady."

Margaret felt her knees turn weak and her heart thump painfully. She could not go through with it. The whole scheme was downright ridiculous. Utter madness!

"Jem says to be quick, my lady," Kitty whispered anxiously.

Margaret whirled away from the mirror, grabbed her white gloves and her fan, and ran lightly down the stairs and out the front door, from which the footmen had been removed after the departure of the earl's party.

5

CHARLOTTE WAS FINDING it very hard to behave as if she were relaxed and enjoying herself. She knew that under any other circumstances she would be enchanted with Vauxhall Gardens. It was a delightful area of trees, grass, and winding avenues, close to the river. All was made excitingly mysterious by the colored lanterns in the trees, colored, moving shadows created by their blowing in the breeze. Music wafted from the orchestra room, and dancers, many masked, moved gaily in the dancing area.

This was one place in London where everyone felt free to come, members of the *ton* rubbing shoulders with cits as they contempuously called the merchant class, and servants and laborers too. Charlotte clung to Devin's arm, fearful of losing her party in the crowd. But he steered them all to a private box he had reserved ahead of time, and they fed again on plates of cold meat, strawberries, and wine.

Charlotte viewed the occupants of the other boxes and recognized many of them. The masks that most of them wore had not been intended to disguise their identities, but only to add a dash of romance to their appearance.

But Charlotte's heart was not in the entertainment. As she chatted with Devin and the earl and occasionally with Lady Lucy and Sir Henry, she played nervously with her fan and tried to estimate when an hour would be passed. By that time Margaret should be there.

Finally she judged it was time. She got to her feet impatiently and turned to Devin.

"It is just too heavenly here to be sitting in one spot all evening," she said, giving him a flirtatious slap on the wrist with her fan. "Pray, let us walk, Mr. Northcott."

He was on his feet in a moment, gallantly offering his arm.

"Sir Henry and Lady Lucy?" she queried, turning in their direction.

But they were enjoying each other's company too much and declined the exercise.

"Lord Brampton?" Charlotte asked, the blood pounding in her ears. A great deal depended on his reply.

"Whichever couple I join," he said ruefully, "I shall feel decidedly *de trop*. However, I do believe I shall walk. If you and Dev are really fortunate, Charlotte, you may lose me along one of these dim paths."

"But we have no intention of losing you, my lord," Charlotte replied, and she linked her free arm through his. Had the occasion not been such an anxious one, she thought, she would have felt remarkably pleased with herself to be seen walking between two such distinguished-looking masked gentlemen.

Meanwhile Jem had maneuvered the plain town carriage into a secluded parking space outside Vauxhall Gardens and had lowered the steps for her ladyship to alight. He was surprised that Kitty had allowed her mistress to leave without a cloak. The night was warm, but not warm enough for bare arms, he reflected. However, there was no accounting for the whims of the Quality. This whole escapade seemed strangely mad to him. Like all the servants of the Earl of Brampton, though, both in London and at Brampton Court, he had fast acquired a fierce loyalty to the countess. With all her quiet and gentle ways, she treated the servants with unfailing courtesy and knew them as individuals. She never failed to inquire after Chalmer's gout, or to ask the scullery maid if she had recovered from her cold, or to comment on the youngest footman's new livery.

Margaret was nervous as she climbed down from the coach. She could never remember being out alone before and the night seemed unusually dark. She was very glad of Jem's presence as she entered the gardens and began to walk along the avenues. He walked a respectful distance behind her, but the distance closed rapidly on the two occasions when her solitary figure drew the attention of some masked gallants. Jem, about as tall and as broad as his master, made a menacing figure in his dark-gray cloak and mask.

It seemed that they wandered for a long while. One problem that Charlotte and Margaret had never been able to solve was arranging a definite rendezvous. Neither they nor Kitty knew the place. All they did know was that there was an orchestra room there. They had therefore made vague plans to walk in that general area and hope that their paths eventually crossed.

It seemed to Margaret that she would have to give up and go home. The area was just too large. There were too many paths and too many people. But suddenly she heard a cough from behind and Jem's voice directed quietly, "To your left, my lady."

And there they were, the three of them strolling

toward her, still a distance away. Margaret judged that even Charlotte had not seen her yet. She moved quickly off the path into the shadows of the bordering trees. Jem had disappeared entirely.

Now that the moment was upon her, Margaret felt that she must faint, for the first time in her life. How could she have been mad enough to allow Charlotte to draw her into this scheme? In another moment he would see her. He would instantly recognize her. And how was she to explain her presence and her strange appearance when she was supposed to be at home in bed, in a laudanum-induced sleep? She still did not have any story prepared for him.

If she did not do it now, she decided desperately, she would lose all courage and never do it. She drew a steadying breath and stepped out into the path.

They were closer than she had expected. Devin was staring up into the treetops, Richard had his head bent to hear something that Charlotte was saying. Margaret stood still, waving her fan slowly in front of her face, looking over its top. Richard looked up.

She had never really expected him to remember her. Her greatest hope was that if she used the flirtatious manner, his interest would be aroused and some subconscious memory would be stirred. Her greatest fear was that he would take no notice of her at all, or—worse!—that he would look on her with amusement or contempt. She certainly was not prepared for his actual reaction.

His whole body froze. Charlotte was almost jerked off her feet with the sudden cessation of movement. Margaret, watching his face intently, could not decipher the expression in his eyes. Her view was hampered by his black mask. But his lips formed a word. She was in no doubt that that word was "angel." Then she fluttered her fan more briskly, turned on her heel, and began to walk swiftly down the path away from him, swinging her wide skirts with provocative movements of her hips.

The Earl of Brampton was in shock for a few moments. He thought he was having a hallucination. There she was before him, surely, exactly as he remembered her—his little angel of the Hetheringtons' masquerade ball. That vivacious little figure would be etched on his memory for all time. He had not been able to explain to himself the almost uncontrollable attraction he had felt for the girl whose name he did not know and whose face he had not been able to see. All he did know was that what had started as a delightful flirtation in the ballroom had changed into sudden passion in the garden, and that by the time he had brought her back to the terrace for a drink of lemonade, his heart was quite smitten. He had meant it when he told her that he would be calling on her. Richard Adair, who had not once thought about matrimony in connection with himself, was hearing wedding bells as he skirted the ballroom and made his way to the refreshment room. But when he had returned with the glass of lemonade, as excited as any boy, he had found that she had disappeared.

His manner had become more and more frenzied during the next half-hour as he searched for her in every likely place and even in some unlikely places. When he had asked about her, deliberately keeping his manner cool and almost bored, he had discovered that though several people remembered Marie Antoinette, no one knew who she was and no one had seen whom she had come with or left with.

For the rest of that Season Brampton had searched for her. He had attended every social function to which he was invited, to the amazement of his friends, and had danced and conversed with every small girl that he saw. But he had felt instinctively that none was she. Once he had even danced a quadrille with Margaret Wells; but his attention had wandered away from her after only a minute. This quiet, dull little girl did not resemble his angel in anything but size.

At the end of the Season, when most of the members of the *ton* had drifted to Brighton or to their family estates for the summer, Brampton had finally admitted defeat. He would never see her again, never hold her light little body again, never make love to her. From that time he developed a taste for voluptuous mistresses. They reminded him less of what he had lost. These thoughts occupied Brampton's mind for a mere few seconds as he stood mesmerized in Vauxhall Gardens, Charlotte clinging to his arm and staring inquiringly up at him.

Then the apparition flirted her fan at him and began to hurry away. It could not be she, of course. But Brampton yielded to the feeling of panic he experienced as she moved away from him. He had to talk to her.

He glanced hastily across to Devin. "Dev, escort Miss Wells back to the box, please, and rejoin Lucy and Henry. I—I have to greet an acquaintance."

And he hurried after the masked figure, who was glancing over her shoulder before turning into a different path.

Devin's mouth was hanging open. He was bewildered. "What the devil?" he said, forgetting to suit his language to his company. "That's Lady Bram."

"Ohh!" Charlotte's hand shot to her mouth and she regarded Devin with wide eyes of dismay. "Is it so obvious?"

He looked at her suspiciously. "Have the feeling

there's something fishy going on," he said. "What's brewing, Miss Wells?"

"It's a long story, sir," she replied meekly.

He took her arm and pulled it firmly through his again. "A long way back to the box," he said sternly. "Better start talking."

Margaret felt a firm hand on her arm soon after she had turned into a wider avenue. She turned to face him, her fan in front of her nose, her eyes sparkling above it.

"Are you?" he asked, puzzled, searching her eyes closely.

"Am I what, monsieur?" she asked, using the husky voice and the French accent that she had used on that previous occasion.

"By Jove, you are she," he exclaimed, and putting his free hand on her other arm, he turned her to face him. The pale-blue light of a lantern gave her mask and gown an even more ethereal quality and darkened her eyes.

"Yes, monsieur," she murmured.

They continued to gaze into each other's eyes for several moments. Then Brampton gave himself a mental shake.

"And are you about to disappear into thin air again as you did last time?" he asked, gripping her arms more tightly.

"Ah, monsieur, I could not stay that time. I told you that I was in grave danger, n'est-ce pas?"

"But to disappear so completely for six years! Did you know that I searched and searched for you? But you were nowhere to be found." His voice softened and his eyes wandered to her mouth, which looked soft and inviting. "Where did you go, and where have you been ever since, my little angel?"

"That I cannot reveal, monsieur," she said. "But you see, I am here now, and let me see"—she spread her fan and examined its dark-red surface—"I have the next six dances free. What coincidence, no?" She glanced up at him through her eyelashes and smiled dazzlingly.

"Minx!" he said, drawing one of her hands through his arm, but keeping a firm grip on it with his other hand. "Come, this is no place to talk. Let us try another path."

He drew her along a narrower walk, not so well lit. They walked until he spotted one of the little rustic shelters that were dotted throughout the gardens. They were furnished with simply designed tables and benches for the convenience of guests who wished to eat *tête-à-tête*.

Brampton ascertained that it was not occupied and drew his companion inside. He did not take with him the lantern that was hanging from a convenient tree branch outside.

He did not make use of the bench. He placed his back against one wall of the shelter and drew Margaret against him, his hands spread across her back. She drew in an unsteady breath.

"I still do not quite believe this, angel," he said. "Is this an accidental meeting? It looked planned."

Margaret's brain whirled in alarm. "Monsieur," she said, "I was with some people and I saw you—with the green lady, no? But I think the green lady was more *enchantée* with the small man. I remembered you, monsieur, and I wished to—talk to you. So I give my companions—how you say?—the slips, *n'est-ce pas?*"

She could see the flash of Brampton's grin in the dark. She lightly tossed her fan and her gloves on the table behind her and rested her hands against his chest, her fingers spread wide. The grin disappeared.

"Little one," he said softly, "do not deny me this time. Remove your mask for me." And he raised one hand and took off his own, sending it to join Margaret's belongings on the table.

"Ah, do not ask it of me, monsieur," she begged. "Truly, you must not know my identity."

"Oh, but I must," he coaxed, moving his head down so that only an inch of space separated their lips. "I have waited for this for six years, angel."

"Please, monsieur, you will give me much distress if you insist," Margaret pleaded, raising large, tear-filled eyes to his.

He sighed. "I see you mean to tease me for six more years," he said. "But come, my little sweet, give me something by which to remember this meeting."

He did not move forward to cover that inch of space. He waited for her to do so. Margaret touched her husband's lips hesitantly with her own, and then they both groaned as his arms clasped her tightly to him and his mouth opened and pressed demandingly down on hers.

Margaret gasped in shock. Time had softened the memory of that first kiss so that the remembered passion had lost its physical impact. Memory rushed back now as she felt the reality of his hard, muscled arms against her back, her breasts crushed against his strong chest, her thighs feeling the heat of his through the fabric of their clothing.

And she discovered again the wildly unexpected delight of his mouth, warm and moist, tasting faintly of the wine he had been drinking. Then his tongue was in her mouth, exploring the surface of her tongue, then moving lightly over the back of her teeth, and finally plunging slowly in and out in imitation of the sexual act.

Margaret felt herself grow hot all over and she became aware of a slow erotic throbbing low in her womb. One of her hands moved upward to entwine in his thick hair; the other splayed across his back, exploring the rippling muscles.

Brampton broke the seal of their mouths after a long time and his head moved down to her neck and throat, his mouth and tongue blazing a hot, moist trail over her bare flesh and down to the deep decolletage of her dress. She arched against him with a low sigh, her one hand pulling his head even closer to her.

One of his hands moved to the row of small buttons at the back of her gown. Then the other hand joined it and he began to undo the buttons until the dress was loosened to the waist. He held her away from him and gazed into her passion-heavy eyes while he slipped the bodice of her gown away from her figure. She wore nothing underneath. In the faint light that filtered through the doorway, Brampton found himself gazing at small but perfectly formed, upward-tilting breasts, the nipples already hard with desire. He cupped a hand reverently beneath each breast and teased the nipples gently with circling thumbs. The expression in her eyes became even more remote.

He lowered his head and licked lightly at each hardened tip. Margaret moaned in an agony of desire.

"My sweet little angel," he murmured against her ear, his hands placing her breasts gently against his silk coat and then moving to her back, "I have loved you for so long. I must have you. Now. Please."

Margaret was shocked into immobility. Not by the attempted seduction. But by the rest of what he had said. His hands were undoing the buttons below her waist. His mouth was seeking hers again.

"No, no, monsieur!" she cried, one hand going behind her back to prevent his activity there, the other hand pushing at his chest. "Please, no!"

"Oh, yes, little one, yes," he insisted, still trying to capture her mouth with his.

"Monsieur, please!" she pleaded, in a real panic now. "Someone may come. Your people will be looking for you. My friends will have missed me!"

"Please, my angel."

"But please, no, monsieur!"

With a great effort Brampton forced himself to relax against the wall behind him. He held her loosely against him. Damn, but the little apparition was right. In another minute he would have had her naked on the floor beneath him, in an almost public place! He had quite taken leave of his senses.

"I am sorry, my sweet," he said, fighting to regain control over himself. And he moved her away from him, helped her on with the bodice of her dress, and turned her around so that he could fasten the buttons again. He slid his arms around her waist from behind, kissed the back of her neck, and drew her against him.

"I am afraid to let you go, my angel," he said softly. "You will disappear again and I shall not know where to look for you or for whom to look."

"Are you sure that you wish to see me again?" Margaret asked, unconsciously holding her breath.

He groaned. "Now that I have found you again, I do not know how I have lived without you," he said.

"I shall come here again one week from tonight. Will you too be here, monsieur?" she asked, slanting a provocative look back over her shoulder.

"Nothing could keep me away, angel," he said. "But how can I be sure you will not disappear into thin air?"

"I give you my promise, monsieur," she swore.

"Tell me who you are," he whispered.

She took his hands in hers and unclasped them from her waist. She picked up her fan and gloves and turned to face him.

"*Au revoir*, monsieur," she said, and she tapped him lightly on one shoulder with the fan, flashed her eyes and teeth at him in a gay smile, and whisked her skirts out through the doorway. She stole a glance back over her shoulder as she sped lightly down the path to the more brightly lit avenue. He was standing in the doorway of the shelter, but was making no attempt to follow her.

She was too emotionally disturbed to be surprised when she noticed soon that Jem *was* following her, at the same respectful distance as before.

6

BRAMPTON WAS GALLOPING his horse in Hyde Park as fast as safety would allow. It was too early in the day for his progress to be impeded by carriages or pedestrians, or even by many other riders. It was too early for Devin Northcott; the two men met in the park quite frequently by unspoken agreement and enjoyed a talk while their mounts cantered over the grass.

For half an hour his mind was too full for coherent thought. He gave himself up to the sensations of the ride, the cool, early-morning mist whipping a flush of color to his cheeks.

He still felt his elation from the discovery of the night before. After six years he had found his angel again, and she sparkled with as much mischief and as much passion as she had on that first meeting. Brampton realized that he had never stopped loving her. Her tiny body had fitted itself to his powerful frame as if he had held her only the day before. He thought of her lips, her mouth, the smooth white skin of her throat, her firm, perfect little breasts. He remembered the way her hips and thighs had molded themselves provocatively against his as he had touched his tongue to her nipples.

She was his! She had to be his! He realized all the absurdity of loving a woman whose face he had never seen and whose identity he did not know. Was her face ugly? Was that why she was so reluctant to show it? But no, no woman with such sparkling eyes and such seductive lips could be ugly. And he felt that he would not have cared even if her face did not prove as beautiful as promised. Her beauty lay all in the perfect little body and the life and passion that sang from it.

He loved her! He dug the spurs into his horse's sides and increased the speed of his gallop. He must see her again. What would he do if she failed to appear the following week? He refused to consider the possibility. She must be there! And he must have somewhere to take her so that he could unclothe the tiny little form, remove the wig and the mask, and feast his eyes and his body on her beauty. To make love to her was now the one urgent goal of his life.

He had to admit to a twinge of uneasiness, though. Why had she suddenly appeared, dressed exactly as she had been six years before? He could not believe it an accident. Her story did not quite ring true. Even if she had spoken part of the truth, was it likely that she would have recognized him, masked and cloaked as he was, after six years? And what would have happened if his wife had been with him, as she would have been but for the sudden headache? There was some puzzling mystery here, but Brampton found that the mystery only heightened his desire to see his angel again.

He galloped the length of the park again before admitting that something was threatening to dull his excitement. His wife! Had he turned unfaithful to her so soon after his vow to make theirs a marriage in deed? Would he be able to betray her when she performed her part of the marriage so sweetly and so uncomplainingly? Her large eyes always looked into his with a quiet trust. Would he be able to meet those eyes after last night, especially with the knowledge that he was scheming for physical union with the other woman? Would he be able to go to his wife's bed without feeling that he was sullying her unresisting, yet sweetly warm little body?

It was only at that moment that Brampton realized the remarkable similarity between the two women in his life. So alike in body, yet so vastly different in manner!

He noticed that his horse had begun to lather. Brampton felt a pang of guilt; he usually treated his horses with unfailing consideration. He turned its head for the stables at home.

Margaret was sitting alone at the breakfast table when Brampton entered, still in his riding clothes. He looked into her face, but avoided her eyes. He felt strangely embarrassed. But he did notice that she looked paler than usual.

"Good morning, my dear," he said. "Do you still have the headache?"

"Yes, Richard," she replied, thankful that he had turned to the sideboard to fill a plate with food. She found it equally difficult to meet his eyes. "I did not sleep well." At least she was not forced to lie this morning, she thought with wry humor.

"Did you not take the laudanum?" he asked, frowning.

"I am afraid it did not take effect," she replied, avoiding the question. "But I shall be fine presently. Charlotte has promised to walk in the park with me."

"Better still, you will drive there," he said, "and with me."

Margaret looked up from her coffeecup in surprise. She would not have expected such an offer on any morning, but especially not on this particular morning.

"Did you enjoy yourself last night?" she asked, watching his bent head closely. He showed no visible reaction.

"I felt like a wallflower." He glanced up and smiled. "I should have felt more comfortable with you there, my dear."

"I thought you would have met plenty of acquaintances there," Margaret quizzed, reluctant to drop the subject.

"Yes, but you had delegated the position of chaperon to me," he said, still smiling, though she fancied that the smile was rather tight. "I was not at liberty to pursue masked figures and guess identities." And he winced inwardly at his choice of words, which only accentuated his deception.

"My dear, why don't I send a message to Dev to see if he would wish to make up a party of four to drive out of the city? We could have a picnic luncheon made up. Would Charlotte enjoy the treat? And would you?"

"Why, Richard, how lovely that would be," Margaret said in surprise, and Brampton noticed that for once she had color in her cheeks and her eyes glowed. "I must go wake Charlotte."

"Shall we say one hour from now?" Her husband smiled.

A few minutes later Margaret left a sleepily grumbling Charlotte and returned to her own room, where she rang for Kitty and tried to decide what to wear for the day. She decided upon a simple primrose-yellow muslin gown with a bonnet to match. Kitty drew a tan-colored pelisse out of the closet, insisting that the day was not yet warm

enough for her mistress to go outside without a
cloak.

Margaret refused to let Kitty dress her hair in any
other style but the tight braids coiled at the back of
her head; she was soon ready and dismissed her
maid. She sat in a chair by the window to wait for the
hour to pass.

Richard had taken her by surprise this morning.
She had expected him to be preoccupied, to almost
totally ignore her for the next week. Yet he was
showing her unexpected attention. His manner at the
breakfast table had seemed genuinely concerned,
almost as if he really cared.

For a while after she had returned home the night
before, Margaret had sat on the edge of her bed, the
wig and the mask beside her, reliving the events of
the last few hours. She had recaptured in her imagination every word he had said, every caress he had
given. How she loved him and how alive and desir-
able he had made her feel! She had not known it
possible that mere touches and kisses could arouse
in her such an aching desire. She had wanted him as
much as he had seemed to want her. She would have
allowed him to finish undressing her; she had been
almost frantic with the need to feel him in her,
bringing ease to her throbbing ache of desire. But his
words had startled her back to an awareness of
reality.

"I have loved you for so long," he had said.

Margaret had longed for six years to hear him say
those words, but had not dreamed that she ever
would. Richard loved her and he wanted her!

Margaret had shivered on the bed, leapt to her feet,
and begun to undress hastily. Was she mad? He
might be at home any moment. She did not believe

that he would visit her that night, but there was always the chance that he might check to see that she slept peacefully. He must not find any trace of her costume.

When everything had been safely stowed away at the back of a closet, Margaret had quickly brushed and braided her hair and climbed into bed. She had told Kitty not to wait up for her.

She had lain in the darkness, feeling a sudden wave of sadness wash over her. Richard did not love her. He loved a faceless phantom without identity. If he knew that it was Margaret that he hungered for, he would turn from her in disgust. He would realize that there was no such person as his angel; that he had been tricked by his dull, unattractive wife. He would hate her then, wouldn't he? He would never want to touch her again. She would lose even the little of him that she now had.

She had felt rather sick too when she remembered the ease with which she had been able to draw his attention. He would have made love to her, believing her to be a stranger. He had made an assignation to see her the following week. And he had believed that he had a wife at home. She had always realized that he must have mistresses, that he slept with other women as well as with her. But this very real evidence that she was right left a sick feeling of depression in her stomach. It was small consolation that this time he was planning to be unfaithful *with* his own wife.

Should she meet him the following week? Strangely enough, neither she nor Charlotte had looked this far ahead in their plans. All they had thought of was deceiving Richard and finding out if she still had the power to attract him in the costume of Marie Antoinette and with the voice and the manner that she had used on that other occasion. Somehow, both had seemed to dream that at the end of a romantic reunion, Margaret's mask would be whisked aside, they would declare undying love for each other, and live happily ever after. At least, that had been Charlotte's dream. Margaret had refused to believe that she would make any impact on Richard at all.

She had still been trying to decide what to do the following week when there had been a tap at the bedroom door. Her heart had turned over, though that was not the entrance usually used by her husband. The door had opened quietly and Charlotte had entered, carrying a candle. She had still been wearing the green domino, and her mask had dangled from her free hand.

"Meg, you were wonderful," she had whispered with enthusiasm. "He did not suspect a thing, did he?"

"No, he did not know me," Margaret had confirmed.

"But he was gone such a long while. What happened, Meg?"

Margaret was certainly not going to answer that one truthfully. "He wanted to know who I was," she had replied vaguely. "He remembered me, and wants to see me again."

"Then he *is* interested. Oh, Meg!" Charlotte had clasped her hands in ecstasy. "Did he kiss you?"

Margaret had hesitated. "Yes, he kissed me."

"Meg! I just knew the two of you were meant for each other. You are going to see him again, are you not?"

"I don't know, Lottie. I think this charade has gone

far enough," Margaret had said firmly, and no amount of coaxing or protesting from her sister had been able to change her mind.

"Oh, Meg," Charlotte had said finally, "Mr. Northcott knows."

"What?"

"He recognized you immediately, Meg, and I was forced to tell him the whole story."

"Lottie!"

"Oh, he promised not to breathe a word to Lord Brampton," Charlotte hastened to assure her sister, "and he promised to help if he could."

"Lottie!"

"I am sorry, Meg," Charlotte said in a small voice. "But if I had said it was not you, you see, he would surely have gone after Lord Brampton to see what was going on."

Margaret had covered her face with her hands, overpowered by humiliation and doubly determined that this mad escapade must end.

On the morning after, though, as she sat at the window waiting for the appointed time for the picnic, she knew that she would don that costume one more time the following week and go to Vauxhall to keep her tryst with Richard. She had to know just once what it would be like to have him make real love to her. And she knew without a doubt that that was what would happen the following week. After that, she would be contented to resume her married life as she had known it so far. Richard's angel would die a natural death.

They drove up into the hills north of the city, the ladies in an open landau, a wicker picnic hamper on the seat opposite them, the men riding alongside. Margaret found the day to be a delightful interlude in a life that kept her apart from her husband a great deal. He and Devin Northcott rode close to the carriage, carrying on a gay conversation, mainly with Charlotte, who looked her best in a sky blue high-waisted dress and darker-blue pelisse and bonnet.

They stopped for lunch on a delightful grassy slope that overlooked the city of London. Brampton's cook had packed them a meal of chicken pieces, lobster patties, bread rolls, cheese, eggs, salad, jellies, and cakes—and bottles of wine.

Devin was the first to rise from the blanket on which they all sat.

"Lady Brampton, would you care to walk?" he asked, bowing in her direction and extending his arm.

Margaret felt embarrassed, knowing that he was aware of her adventure of the night before, but her usual calm demeanor came to her aid. She rose to her feet and took his arm. They walked slowly up the slope away from the panoramic view.

"Is your headache better, ma'am?" he began.

"Yes, thank you, Mr. Northcott, but I believe you know that was a piece of deception," she replied calmly.

He gave her a sidelong glance and coughed delicately. "Quite so, ma'am," he agreed. "Afraid I forced the story out of Miss Wells."

"That is quite all right, sir," Margaret said, "but I would beg of you not to breathe a word of the matter to my husband." She kept her face pointing forward, feeling the color rising to her cheeks.

"Wouldn't dream of doing any such thing, ma'am," he replied, eyebrows raised, "and wouldn't be so indelicate as to raise the matter now. But felt you should know one thing." Devin coughed again.

Margaret looked inquiringly into his face. "Yes?" she prompted.

"Bram ain't usually into this sort of thing," Devin said, reddening himself. "Females, I mean. Not since his marriage, that is."

"Pray do not trouble yourself, sir," Margaret cut in hastily. "I do not pry into Richard's private life."

"No, but that's the point, ma'am," Devin said earnestly. "Ain't been anything to pry into."

"Until now?"

"Until now, ma'am. And I b'lieve he's drawn to you now just because it's you, if you know what I mean, though he don't know it himself."

They continued their walk in silence for a while as Margaret digested what he had been saying to her. She could hear the approaching voices of Charlotte and her husband.

"Thank you, Mr. Northcott," she said, smiling up at him.

"M' pleasure, ma'am," he replied seriously.

"You two look like a staid old couple," Charlotte called gaily. They looked back to see her approaching with Lord Brampton.

"Come, Mr. Northcott," Charlotte said, taking the arm that Margaret was relinquishing, "let us see if we can spot St. Paul's Cathedral from the top of this rise." And they moved ahead at a brisk pace.

Margaret took Brampton's proffered arm.

"Are you feeling more the thing, my dear?" he asked.

"Yes, thank you, Richard," she replied with a placid smile.

They walked together in companionable silence, viewed the city with the others, and started on their way back to the carriage and the horses. Margaret noticed the way Charlotte clung to Devin Northcott's arm and the animated way in which she talked to him. She noticed the warmth of his smile as he listened to and replied to her sister.

Was Charlotte spending too much time with Devin Northcott? Margaret wondered. Only a few weeks before, she had had great dreams of introducing her sister to the *ton*, of ensuring that she met a large number of eligible young men. Margaret hoped that her sister would make a sound love match within the next year or two. She did not wish to see her sister suffer the years of pain and loneliness that she had suffered. And Charlotte had been quite a hit. A number of young men came to call on her and take her driving in the park; Charlotte never lacked for partners at a ball.

But somehow Mr. Northcott had come to be her accepted regular escort. And Margaret wondered if she and Richard were responsible for that. It was very convenient to have Richard's closest friend as a partner for her sister. But was it a good thing for Charlotte? Devin Northcott must be almost of an age with Richard, certainly well over a decade older than Charlotte.

Margaret came to the conclusion that she had been so preoccupied with her own affairs in the last few weeks that she had been neglecting her duties as chaperone to her sister. She must redouble her efforts to see that Charlotte met more eligible young men from her own age group.

As the earl, Margaret, and Charlotte entered the house on Grosvenor Square late in the afternoon, Chalmer met them in the hallway with the news that the Dowager Countess of Brampton and Lady Rosalind Crowthers were awaiting their return in the drawing room.

"Mama?" Brampton asked, his eyebrows raised in some surprise. "What the devil does she want at this hour?"

Chalmer tactfully ignored the question, but climbed the stairs ahead of his master and mistress to open the door to the drawing room on the first floor. Charlotte retreated to her own room.

"And Rosalind too," Brampton commented to his wife. "Something's up."

The dowager was sitting stiffly on a sofa when they entered the room. Rosalind was hovering over her, vinaigrette in hand.

"Richard, dear," his mother said faintly, "where ever have you been? Good day, Margaret, my love."

"Had I known you were planning to pay us a visit, Mama," Brampton said dryly, "I should have been sure to be here."

"Richard, if you just knew what poor, dear Mama has to suffer, you would not talk with such a note of levity," Rosalind scolded.

"Have you had tea brought up?" Margaret asked soothingly. "I shall ring immediately."

"No, no, my love, I should choke on it," the dowager replied tragically. "Richard, dear, it's poor Charles."

Brampton paled noticeably. "Charles?" he said. Margaret moved swiftly to his side and put a steadying hand on his arm. His other hand covered it.

"I begged you, Richard dear, not to buy him his commision. He was ever a delicate boy. But no one ever listened to me or cared for my delicate sensibilities. Well, perhaps now you will be sorry that you did not pay heed to your mother."

"Mama," Brampton said harshly, unconsciously squeezing Margaret's fingers in a painful grip, "what has happened to Charles?"

"And why the Duke of Wellington has not finished with Boney's men once and for all instead of chasing them all over Spain, I shall never know," his mother continued, sniffing against a lace handkerchief.

"Mama!"

"Poor dear Charles has been wounded and is being sent home to die, I would not doubt," the dowager announced.

Margaret felt her husband take a deep and ragged breath.

"Sit down, my lord," she said, trying to draw him across to the nearest chair.

He shook off her arm and faced his mother wild-eyed. "To die?" he queried.

"Well, the poor boy says a bone in his arm has been shattered by a ball, but that he is in no danger. But I have heard about these field surgeons, Richard dear, and I know what butchers they are. I would not doubt that the wound will turn putrid and they will have to cut off the arm and he will die. And he has had the fever, poor boy, so that he is too weak to follow the army about Spain. So they are sending him home to die." The dowager collapsed, weeping into her handkerchief.

"Pray, do not take on so, Mama," Rosalind soothed while Brampton straightened up, looking visibly relieved.

"You have a letter from Charles, Mama?" he asked, holding out a hand.

She felt inside her reticule and drew out a crumpled sheet of paper. She handed it to her son and he perused it quickly.

"It is all right, my dear," he said, turning to Margaret, who still stood at his shoulder. "He is being given invalid leave, but only because the army is constantly traveling and his wound does not allow him to be of any use to his regiment. He is in no danger."

Margaret smiled at him and touched his arm again shyly. "I am glad, Richard," she said. "I shall look forward to meeting my brother-in-law."

"Dear Charles hopes to be at home within the week," his mother added. "Come, Rosalind, I have a great many preparations to make. I must make sure that the bed is ready for my poor boy."

Handkerchief, vinaigrette, and reticule were swept together and the ladies took their leave. Margaret was left wondering how her sister would react to a regimental uniform.

7

CAPTAIN CHARLES ADAIR arrived home four days later. He refused to take to the bed his mother had so painstakingly prepared for him. He did allow himself to be examined by the physician she had lined up for the occasion, but only to set her mind at rest. Then he summoned his older brother, and the two sallied forth to White's Club.

On the following evening, the Earl and Countess of Brampton gave a dinner in honor of Captain Adair's safe return home. Margaret spent longer than usual in her dressing room getting ready for the evening. She knew that Richard had not married her for love, and she knew that she was not an attractive woman. But she wanted to make a favorable impression on her brother-in-law. She did not want him to feel that his brother had married a dowd.

She wore a dress of pale-blue lace over a white silk underdress. She had Kitty dress her braids higher than usual on her head. Her only ornaments were a pearl necklace that Richard had given her as a wedding gift, and her wedding rings.

Margaret was one of the last to enter the drawing room. Her mother-in-law was there already, holding court to Devin Northcott and another, elderly gentleman. Her two sisters-in-law who were in town were also present with their husbands. There were several other close acquaintances, talking in groups. But Margaret's attention was caught by the three central figures before the fireplace. Richard was looking his usual magnificent and immaculate self, dressed in black, the color relieved only by his snowy-white shirt and flowing neckcloth. Charlotte was looking vivid in a rose-pink dress, her auburn hair dressed in a froth of curls, her cheeks flushed with color.

And Charles—it must be he!—was quite a breathtaking man. He was slightly taller than his brother, though slighter in build, and somewhat sallow of complexion since his bouts of fever in Spain. His hair was fairer and more wavy than his brother's. He bore himself with military straightness and wore full-dress regimentals, his right arm carried in a sling. His face, Margaret noticed as she met his eyes across the room, was open and friendly. She wanted more than ever to be liked by him.

Brampton crossed the room to take her hand and lead her forward. "My dear," he said, "come and meet your brother-in-law, Charles. Charles, my wife."

Charles was feeling a shock of surprise. The countess was unlike anything he had imagined. When he had received news of the marriage, in Spain, he had amused himself trying to picture Dick's bride. Would he have married an acclaimed beauty, someone he would be proud to show off at all the social functions of the *ton?* Or would he have married an uninteresting girl who would give him an heir? He doubted that Dick would have married for love. As Charles remembered him, he had always had need of many women, one at a time, it was true, but none retaining his attention for more than a few months. Charles could not remember having met

Miss Margaret Wells, but her name made her sound as if she fell into the second category of bride.

He was quite unprepared for this fragile little creature who stepped into the room with quiet self-assurance. She was not pretty in any obvious sense of the word, but Charles immediately categorized her as beautiful. Her beauty lay perhaps in the quiet way she bore herself, not using any of the lures he was used to seeing in other women; yet her whole being seemed to shine from her quiet gray eyes, so large and so full of pride in and love of Dick.

Charles looked curiously across at his brother as he made the introductions. By God, he loves her too, Charles decided with amusement. I wonder if he knows it!

"I am enchanted to meet you at last, ma'am," he said, smiling down at this little sister-in-law whom he immediately liked, and with his left hand he raised her hand to his lips.

"Oh, please call me Margaret," she replied. "And I am so happy to meet you too, sir. I never had a brother, you see."

"Then I shall have to make up for lost time, Margaret," he said, laughing. "And it must be Charles, please."

She smiled happily up at him and accepted the left arm he offered to her to lead her into the dining room. She did not notice her husband's eyes fixed, intrigued, on her face before he crossed the room to escort his mother in to dinner.

Margaret had placed Charles to her right, at the foot of the dining table. She had seated Charlotte to his right, hoping that she would not seem too obviously the matchmaker. She watched, satisfied, as they talked together. She hoped that Richard would not object to her sister and his brother developing a *tendre* for each other. She glanced down the table to find her husband's eyes fixed steadily on her as he listened to the chatter of the woman beside him. His expression was unreadable. She smiled placidly at him and turned to the gentleman on her left.

Later, when the gentlemen joined the ladies in the dining room, Brampton noticed that his brother crossed the room to sit between Margaret and Charlotte. They were soon all three deep in conversation, or at least, the two ladies were soon absorbed in listening to Charles. Richard felt the old envy that he had always felt for his brother, who found it so easy to charm people of all age groups. Why was he never able to bring that look of near-animation to his wife's face?

And why should I care? he thought, giving himself a mental shake. He had made a good bargain when he had married her. She was quiet and undemanding. He could forget that she was there if he wanted to. And he certainly had not wanted a woman who would disturb his life in any way. It was fortunate for him that she did not find him as attractive as she seemed to find his brother. She might become a nuisance if she did, demanding what he was not prepared to give. He felt a fresh wave of irritation wash over him as his wife—and Charlotte—broke into peals of laughter over something Charles had said. He had never been able to make her laugh.

And then he remembered what had never really been out of his mind for the last six days: tomorrow night he was to see his angel again! This thought had, in fact, been an agony to him all week. Several times he had made a definite decision not to go. His search for her, the pain he had felt six years before at not being able to find her, was long in the past. Would it not be best to leave it there, to let her slip out of his life again before his feelings were irrevocably involved? At these times he thought of his responsibilities as head of his family. Then he thought of his wife, whom he now held in respect, if not, indeed, in affection. Was he willing to risk the peace and tranquillity of his present life for a romantic gambol with an unidentified figure from his past?

But at other times he admitted to himself that it was already too late. He had held the girl in his arms. She was no phantom, but very real flesh and blood. And he remembered the way passion had flared between them on both occasions. He had to hold her again. He had to have her! He looked forward to the following night with dread, with excitement, and with anxiety.

"Look as if you'd lost your best friend, Bram," said Devin, cutting in on his thoughts.

Brampton was recalled to the present, and to his duties as a host, with a start.

"Seems to have a way with the ladies," Devin continued, nodding in the direction of Charles Adair. "How long d'you say his leave was, Bram?"

Lord Brampton was riding early again in the park next morning. He had already galloped the length of the park and back again before he saw Devin Northcott turn his horse in through the gates. Brampton cantered toward him.

" 'Morning, Bram. You're early," Devin greeted his friend. "Must have something on your conscience."

They rode side by side for a while, talking about trivialities.

Finally Brampton cleared his throat. "Dev, I have a favor to ask of you."

"Anything you ask," Devin replied, watching a young maidservant out walking a dog, and thinking of a head of auburn curls nodding close to a red regimental coat for a whole evening.

"I wish the use of your rooms tonight," Brampton said.

"Eh?"

"I need privacy for certain—business."

Devin was back in the present. "Into the muslin company again, Bram?"

"She is a lady," his friend replied stiffly.

"Mm, yes, quite," Devin commented, and then, on sudden inspiration, "Not the little silver lady from Vauxhall, Bram?"

Brampton did not reply immediately. "Yes," he admitted finally.

Devin gave his friend a sidelong glance. What the devil? Was it really possible that he did not know?

"Have a date to play cards with Freddie Haversham, anyway," he said. "I'll give the servants the night off. Give you my key."

"Thank you, Dev. You're a true friend," Brampton said with relief.

"Must get back now," Devin said, turning his horse. "Breakfast, y'know." He gave Brampton a level look. "I say, Bram," he said, "not at all fair to Lady Bram, y'know."

"Damn it, Dev," Brampton flared. "I do not need you for a conscience. I have a powerful enough one of my own."

Devin Northcott was smiling rather grimly to himself as he prodded his horse into a gallop.

Margaret found it impossible to concentrate on any of her activities that day. She went shopping with Charlotte late in the morning. Charlotte had been complaining that she was wearing the same clothes too frequently and would soon be labeled as a poor country miss if she wore them once more.

"I declare, Meg," she said crossly the day before, "soon people will see a green bonnet turn into Hyde Park from a half-mile distant and know that it must be me."

They had the carriage drop them on Bond Street and walked its length, visiting the various modiste establishments and milliners. They stopped frequently to talk to various lady acquaintances and curtsied to several gentlemen.

Charlotte also insisted on visiting Hookam's library to exchange a book. "I must have a romantic novel to read tonight, Meg," she said. "We cannot go out, as you have your appointment to keep." She giggled.

Margaret, who usually enjoyed a shopping expedition, felt by the time they reached home that she could have screamed with frustration. The day was rushing by, yet time was crawling. She helped Charlotte carry a few bandboxes into the house; two footmen were directed to carry the rest of the boxes and parcels to Charlotte's room. Margaret was glad that she had had the presence of mind to direct, when Charlotte was not within earshot, that the bills be sent to Richard. He would not mind; he was a most generous man. And she could always suggest that he take the money out of her next quarter's allowance. Her father, on the other hand, would not be at all amused by his younger daughter's extravagance.

Margaret spent some time in her room after luncheon, supposedly resting. She thought about the coming evening and felt sick with worry. Was she not courting disaster to meet him again this night? Was he not bound to recognize her? She did not believe that she could face his fury if he discovered her deception. Margaret had never seen her husband lose his temper, but instinct warned her that she would not want to be on the receiving end if he ever did.

Then she thought again of the expertise with which he had embraced her the previous week and of her own response. She thought of the brief, dispassionate encounters that they shared each night in her bed. And she knew again that she must go, whatever the risk.

The remainder of the afternoon was taken up with a drive in the park with Charles. He arrived unexpectedly, demanding that the ladies accompany him to point out some of the more prominent members of the *ton.*

"It is so long since I have been in London that I fear I might ignore someone that I should know," he explained with his charming smile. "That could mean death to my social reputation."

He need not have feared. All eyes were drawn in admiration to his tall, dashing figure as he drove his curricle skillfully through the heavy traffic in the park, and many people claimed reacquaintance. Charlotte, at his side, sparkled, it seemed to Margaret. The two chattered gaily for the duration of the drive, leaving Margaret to her thoughts. She felt happily convinced that there was a very real attraction between her sister and her husband's brother.

Dinner that evening was a quiet affair. Neither Brampton nor Margaret seemed inclined to make conversation, and Charlotte, for once, seemed wrapped up in thought. Brampton was preoccupied with his guilt and his anticipation of seeing his angel again. Margaret was excited and sick with anxiety.

"I shall be leaving presently, my dear," Brampton announced across the table to his wife. "I have an engagement and shall probably be late."

Margaret smiled placidly. "That is all right, Richard," she said. "Charlotte and I have planned a quiet evening."

"What?" he said, eyebrows raised. "Do you have no invitations for tonight?"

"Yes, two," she replied calmly. "Lady Emberly is having a card party and the Prices a musical soiree. But we have declined both."

"I hope that Charlotte is not becoming bored with the Season already," he said, smiling teasingly at her.

"Oh, no, indeed, my lord," she cried, "but I—I have the headache." Then she bit her lip, remembering that that had been Meg's excuse the week before.

"I am sorry to hear it," Brampton said. "Might I suggest an early night?"

"Yes, my lord, it is exactly what I intended," said Charlotte meekly, eyes on her plate. "And Meg has kindly offered to stay at home to bear me company."

Charlotte was not a convincing actress, but Brampton's mind was only half on the conversation. He accepted her explanations without suspicion.

One hour later, Brampton having departed for his "engagement," Margaret was in her room, yet again being dressed in the silver gown and mask, her hair piled loosely beneath the powdered wig. Both Kitty and Charlotte were present and helping, both as nervous and excited as Margaret herself.

Kitty applied the lip rouge, Margaret slipped her feet into the wine-colored slippers, took the matching fan from Charlotte, and was ready to leave. This time Kitty smuggled her down the back stairs and out through the servants' entrance, so that she would not be observed by the butler and footmen.

Margaret ran lightly across to the stables, where Jem was waiting, the plain carriage ready for her.

"Jem," she said as he helped her inside the carriage and lifted the steps, "please follow me wherever I go tonight. I do not wish to be caught without a conveyance."

Jem could not quite understand why her ladyship needed to arrange a secret meeting with her own husband and why she must return separately from him, but it was not his job to question the Quality, certainly not his master and mistress.

"You need have no fears, your ladyship," he assured her before closing the door. "I shall see that you come safely home."

"Thank you, Jem." She favored him with one of her rare smiles, which won for her his even deeper devotion.

Vauxhall looked more familiar on this occasion, though Margaret felt even more nervous than before. That last time, if Richard had recognized her, she felt that she could somehow have talked her way out of an awkward situation. It could all have been explained as a joke. She could have pretended a wager with Charlotte that he would not recognize her. But this time, things had gone too far. Richard would really feel he had been made a fool of if he discovered the truth now.

She saw him almost immediately, arms crossed on his chest, leaning against a tree beside the path where she had first caught his attention the week before. She shivered with fear for a moment; he looked very tall and almost menacing, with his black domino drawn closely around him and a black mask that covered more of his face than last week's had done. He obviously did not want to be recognized. Then he pushed himself away from the tree and stood straight. He had seen her.

Margaret smiled dazzlingly, fluttering her fan briskly, and forced a spring into her step as she approached him along the path.

"Angel!" he said, reaching out both hands to grasp hers.

"Ah, monsieur, you came," she said brightly, tapping both his outstretched palms lightly with her closed fan.

"Did you doubt I would?"

"But yes, monsieur," she answered pertly. "I know it is 'ard for a man to be faithful to one woman, *n'est-ce pas?*"

"Ah, but it would not be hard to be faithful to you, I think, little wretch," he said, and he grasped her elbow lightly and began to stroll with her down the path in the direction from which she had come.

"Are we to dance, monsieur?" she asked. "I have been granted the permission to waltz. Remember?"

"Do you really wish to dance?" he asked.

"But yes," she said. "It is so lovely to dance beneath the stars, no? With someone special," she added daringly, flirting her fan at him.

Brampton was dazzled. He could not decide whether she was a practiced coquette or a delightful little innocent. He hoped the latter. He had not planned to waste time in the gardens with her. He wanted her alone. But he was willing to humor her; he wanted this night to be a long and a perfect one.

"Come, then, little angel," he said, taking her hand and drawing it through his arm, "let us go see if the orchestra will play a waltz."

The orchestra was playing many waltzes. The

dance was favored by the guests as suited to the romantic outdoor setting and to the masked appearance of many of the revelers, who felt they could relax the strict propriety of their behavior.

Brampton drew his companion into the circle of his arms as one waltz started. He held her closer than he would have dared to in a ballroom. Her breasts, firmly held within the heavy bodice of her gown, brushed tantalizingly against the black fabric of his domino. Her powdered wig tickled his cheek and chin.

She moved lightly, her little body picking up the rhythm of his, so that he felt she was floating in his arms. At first, he whirled her through the steps of the dance, exhilarated by the reality of her presence in his arms. Later, his feet slowed, he steered her to the edge of the dancing area, where they were more in the shadow of the trees, and pulled her more firmly against the hard wall of his body. He felt desire stir in him and lowered his head to brush her lips with his. He felt her inhale sharply.

"Angel," he whispered against her ear, "I do not want to share you with these crowds. Will you come with me?"

"Where do you wish me to go with you, monsieur?" she asked, raising her eyes to his so that he had a sensation of drowning.

"To a quiet place where we can be alone," he answered, gazing back.

"I do not know," she whispered.

"Yes, my little one, you do know," he murmured gently. "We both know why we have returned her tonight. Do we not?"

She held his gaze for a breathless moment. "Yes," she said softly.

"Come," he said, kissing her lightly on the lips again, and he led her in silence down a tree-lined avenue to a different exit from the one at which she had entered. She wondered fleetingly if Jem would be able to follow her, but she was in no state of mind to really care.

Brampton handed his wife into his oh-so-familiar town carriage and directed the coachman to Devin Northcott's chambers before springing in to sit close beside her.

They passed through the lit hallway of the stately old house in which Devin Northcott had his rooms and up to the second story. Brampton took a branched candlestick with them, lighting the candles before they climbed the stairs.

He set it down on the hall stand, unfastened the single button at the throat of Margaret's gray cloak, and slipped it from her shoulders. He threw his own black coat to join it on a nearby chair, and removed his mask. He looked so achingly familiar, dressed in the same black evening clothes he had worn the night before. It was hard for Margaret to believe that he did not know her.

But if she had any doubt on that point, the look in his eyes would have undeceived her. He had certainly never looked at the Countess of Brampton with such smoldering desire.

Brampton held out his hand for hers and led her, without prelude, to a bedchamber. He took the candlestick with him. The light from the candles lit up a large room with heavy, stately furniture, including a big four-poster bed, its blue velvet curtains drawn back, bedclothes turned down to reveal snowy-white sheets and pillowcases. Darker-blue velvet curtains were drawn back from the four windows, so that moonlight helped illuminate the room.

Margaret felt panic growing. This was the point of no return, then. She could not possibly now turn the evening away from its inevitable conclusion. And soon, surely, he would know with whom he was dealing.

Brampton set the candlestick down on the dressing table so that the light from the candles was doubled by the reflections from the mirror.

"Come here, angel," he said, holding out his arms to her.

Margaret was still standing uncertainly just inside the door. She went into his arms and felt them close around her.

"And now," he murmured, smiling into her eyes, "finally, let us get rid of this mask and this wig, my angel. Let me see you."

"Ah, no, monsieur," she said anxiously, pushing against his chest. "Please, I cannot do that."

Brampton tightened his hold on her. "What is it, my sweet?" he coaxed, puzzled. "Do you not trust me? I shall not hurt you or betray you to anyone else, even if you turn out to be Princess Caroline herself." He paused and grinned wickedly. "You are not Princess Caroline, are you, angel? It would be tiresome to have to call you 'Your Highness' while I make love to you."

Margaret laughed at the absurd look on his face. "I shall not answer yes or no, monsieur," she said archly. "But I insist that you must not see me."

He sighed in exasperation. "Angel, will you compromise?" he asked. "If I extinguish the candles and pull the curtains across the windows so that we cannot see a hand before our faces, will you unmask

for me? Please, my sweet?" he begged as she
hesitated. "I cannot make love to you if I cannot at
least *feel* your face and your hair."

"How do you know that I wish you to make love to
me, monsieur?" she asked, tapping him briskly on
the shoulder with the fan that she still clutched.

"I assume, little wretch," he replied, "that when
you step willingly into a bedchamber with a man,
you do not do so in order to discuss the weather or
the state of the nation!"

"Snuff the candles, monsieur, and draw the
curtains," Margaret said. "Then I shall give you my
answer."

He did as he was bid. The result was everything
Margaret could have wished. She could see nothing
whatsoever. Neither could he, apparently. She heard
a thud, followed by an oath, as he found his way back
to her.

"You owe me a 'yes' angel," he said close to her ear
as he reached out to take her arm, "to make up for
the crushed ankle I just acquired."

But he gave her no chance to reply. One hand
reached up and pulled firmly at the wig. The pins
that had held up her own hair came away with it.
Margaret heard Brampton draw in his breath
sharply as her heavy long hair cascaded down over
his arm. The strings of the mask had also come
untied with that one tug at the wig. She felt it fall
away to the floor.

Brampton's body was still not touching hers. He
reached up both hands now and let light fingertips
roam over her face—over her forehead and
cheekbones, down the length of her nose, over her
mouth and her jawline. He pushed his fingertips
lightly into the hair at her temples and let gentle
thumbs follow the line of her eyebrows and then the

lids of her closed eyes. His fingers slid deeper into the warmth of her hair.

Then his lips were on hers, gently, without demand, tasting the sweetness of her. They moved on to her cheeks, her forehead, her eyes, her ears. He paused at her right ear to take the lobe between his teeth and bite it gently as he licked at the tip. Margaret felt herself move away from a world of soft dreams into one of raw desire.

His mouth was back on hers, but open this time, hot, demanding, hard. His tongue penetrated the soft moistness of her mouth and explored and teased its interior. Their bodies were still not touching.

Finally Brampton's hand moved down through her hair to her waist and brought her against him. Margaret felt the blood rush in a surge of heat to her cheeks.

His mouth moved to her ear again. "Angel, you are driving me crazy, do you know that?"

"I think I am a little not quite sane too, monsieur," Margaret managed to gasp out.

Both his hands now were at the fastenings of her dress, working the buttons slowly, one by one, through the loops. While his hands were thus busy, he kissed and teased with his tongue and teeth her neck and her shoulders.

Finally the back of her gown was opened to the hips. Brampton drew it down off her shoulders and arms and moved back from her as it fell rustling to the floor. He knew immediately as he reached for her again that she was now naked to the waist. His hands found the small, firm breasts and kneaded them gently as his head came down to take the nipples, one by one, into his mouth. They were soon taut and aching with a throb of desire that trickled downward to her womb. She moaned and arched her hips against him.

"I must have you on the bed, angel," Brampton was whispering against her lips again. He wrapped his arms around her and moved her backward as he kissed her again, until she felt the edge of the bed against the back of her knees. She allowed him to lay her back against the crisp, cool sheets, and moved up so that her head lay on the pillow. She lay still while his hands carefully and knowledgeably removed her shift, her silk stocking, and her undergarments. Finally she lay naked—but unseen—before him for the first time.

He did not join her on the bed immediately. Margaret could hear that he was removing his own clothing. She savored the moment. Her body was singing with awareness of him, already throbbing and aching for fulfillment, more than she had ever experienced in her erotic dreams of him. But she knew there was no need for anxiety. This time he would satisfy her. She would know what it was like to be loved.

Brampton joined her on the bed. He lay beside her, turned toward her but not touching her for the moment. His hand began tracing a light pattern down her body, beginning at her throat and shoulders, moving down over her breasts and rib cage, over her hips and stomach and down the inside of her thighs to her knees. Margaret's breathing quickened and the throbbing of her body became more insistent.

His fingertips came back up the leg closest to him until they reached her stomach again. Then he brought the palm of his hand down on her and began slow, circular movements around her navel.

Margaret half-turned to him, desperate for closer contact.

"Patience, little angel," he said softly, raising himself on one elbow and leaning over her to kiss her slowly and deeply again on the mouth. "Let us make this a loving to remember."

Oh, yes, she would remember this loving, Margaret thought. It would have to last her a lifetime.

His hand moved again until she gasped and pulled away in fright. His fingers had reached down to stroke and caress the warm, moist place between her thighs.

"Do not be frightened, sweet," he murmured against her lips. "I want only to love you." One of his legs hooked around one of hers and drew it toward him; his hand resumed its caresses with greater freedom, his fingernails scratching lightly until Margaret's body was writhing in an agony of throbbing, spiraling longing. She turned and reached for him, blindly.

"Ah, yes, I knew you would be good to love," he said exultantly, firm hands pressing her back down on to the bed again. He moved across her and lowered his weight onto her still-twisting body.

"Oh, please, monsieur. Please. Please!" she gasped, her brain somehow holding on to the deception of the husky French accent.

"Yes, my sweet. Oh yes," he answered, his own voice not quite steady. And then the world stood still as he slid deeply into the soft heat of her. He lay heavily on her for a moment while they both savored the exquisite delight of being joined at last.

Then he raised himself on his forearms, his body a little away from hers, so that he could withdraw himself almost entirely from her before thrusting deeply inside again. Margaret wrapped her legs around his and fit herself to his rhythm as she had in a different way when they had danced earlier. Soon he was driving passionately into her while her desire tightened and tightened and, ultimately, became more and more frightening. She dared not let go. She might lose herself forever.

Brampton felt her inability to climax. He imposed an iron hold on his own almost uncontrollable need to release into her. He slowed his rhythm, let his weight down onto her again, and eased his hands beneath her body.

"What is it, little one?" he murmured.

"I can't. I can't," she gasped, panic-stricken.

"Let me take care of you, angel," he soothed. "I shall hold you safe. Like this, you see? Trust me, sweet. I shall not hurt you."

He coaxed her with deep, slow strokes until she knew she must allow him into the center of her world and she would never be free again.

"I want all of you, angel. Everything you have to give. As I give you my all," he said in a new, harsher, more urgent tone of voice. "Now, darling. Now!"

And he was coming and coming and did not stop coming. Margaret opened the final barrier and exploded against him with shudder after shudder. She was not aware either of her own abandoned cry or of his groan of fulfillment as he followed her into a world of shattering release.

Brampton drew himself out of her and moved his weight away almost immediately, but his arms locked behind her back and took her with him, so that the comforting rock-hardness of his body held her secure for the several minutes during which she could not stop from shaking.

"It was good for you, little one," he said finally, his voice husky with emotion, "as I intended it to be. Sleep now. I shall hold you safe."

Margaret obediently slipped into a sleep of total, delicious relaxation, heedless of the need for caution or the need to leave before dawn should make her face visible.

Brampton lay holding her awhile, before drifting into sleep himself. Now that passion was satisfied, he delighted in the feel of her lovely, firm little body in his arms. Her hair was thick and silky over his arm and against his chest. He wished he could see it, know its color. It reached to her waist.

He rested his cheek against the top of her head and closed his eyes. God, but he wanted this little angel for his own. He had never known such joy as he had just experienced in her arms and still felt in his satiety.

He had had one of his earlier questions answered, at any rate. She was no coquette. He had noticed as soon as he entered her that she was not a virgin. But she certainly lacked experience. Her body had hummed with passion and she had wanted him every bit as much as he had wanted her, but she had made no attempt to make love to him. She had kept her hands to herself, and though she had returned his kisses, she had not initiated any of her own. And at the end she had been terrified of her own response. Obviously, no man had ever taken her to a climax before.

Brampton was glad of that. He had felt momentarily disappointed that she was not a virgin. He would have liked to be her first—and only—man. But that was absurd, of course. Even if she had been a girl when he had first met her, six years would have made her into a woman. And it was unconceivable that such a beautiful, passionate little creature could have remained untouched. Had she had lovers? Was she married? Her fear of revealing her identity suggested that she was. She was probably married to some old fool, he decided with bitter contempt. No real man could have taken this woman's body without awakening it to all the joys of unleashed love and passion. But maybe her husband thought she wanted it that way. And maybe he was right!

But she was made for him. Brampton vowed that he would teach this little angel all the numerous arts and delights of lovemaking that he had learned in his many and varied experiences. He must have her for a long time yet.

Margaret awakened, feeling disoriented. She felt warm, comfortable, safe. She knew immediately that she was not alone. Her cheek was resting against the hard muscles of an arm. The hand belonging to the same arm clasped her shoulder. A heart was beating steadily close to her ear. Richard had not returned to his own room tonight. How delightfully unusual! She snuggled closer to the warmth of his body.

His lips found hers in the darkness and she was suddenly fully awake. She was with Richard, but in an unknown place, and he believed himself to be with a stranger. She sat up in panic. What time was it? How close to daybreak was it?

"I did not mean to sleep, monsieur," she said. "I must go."

He grasped her shoulder and tried to force her back down beside him. "Don't worry, my sweet," he said. "I shall take you home soon. Let me love you once more first."

"Oh, no, no, I must go," she replied, resisting the persuasion of his hand and voice.

"Will you be missed?" he asked with gentle concern.

"I must go," was all she would say.

"Then we will dress and leave," he said soothingly. "It is all right, angel. You will be safe with me."

"Ah, but you must not come with me, monsieur," she said in alarm.

"I shall certainly not allow you out alone in the streets of London at this hour of the night," Brampton declared firmly.

"I have my own carriage, monsieur," Margaret said with far more confidence than she felt. What if Jem had not been able to follow? Or what if he had got tired of waiting and had driven home long before? How would she get home?

"Do you mean that you had my coachman followed?" he asked in amusement. "I begin to see, little minx, how it came about that you escaped Madame Guillotine."

Margaret scrambled off the bed and began the difficult task of gathering her scattered belongings in the darkness. She dressed hastily, wig, mask, and all.

"Angel, when shall I see you again?" Brampton asked from the bed.

Margaret paused.

"I must see you again!" he said urgently.

"I think it would be better not, monsieur," Margaret said sadly. "Nothing can come of this affair."

"But we can love each other, give each other delight—perhaps for a long, long time," he argued.

"You are married, monsieur," she said, heart pounding, "and I do not wish to be any man's mistress."

"And you, angel," he prompted, "are you too married?"

Margaret paused again. "I must leave, monsieur," she said.

"Elusive wretch," he chuckled. "But tell me when I can see you, angel, or I shall get out of this bed and stand before the door until you give me an answer."

"I shall be in the place we met tonight at the same time next week," Margaret replied.

"In Vauxhall?"

"*Oui*, monsieur."

"I shall be there, angel. You will not let me down?"

"You must trust me, monsieur."

He sighed. "I wish you would trust me with your identity."

"Will you promise me," she asked, "not to leave this room for 'alf an hour after I leave?"

"I will promise you the moon and all the stars, angel, if you will just feel your way across to this bed and kiss me again," he replied with another chuckle. Her theatrical air of mystery both intrigued and amused him.

She found her way to his side and bent over him. His arms came viselike around her, toppling her down on top of him. His mouth found hers hungrily and kissed her deeply.

"Ah, you have that glorious hair hidden again," he commented as their lips drew apart. "What color is it, angel?"

"*Au revoir*, monsieur," she said, rising from the bed and feeling her way to the doorway.

Margaret felt terrible fright as she emerged from the house onto the dark, silent street. She knew she would have to go back upstairs to Richard if Jem were not there. She did not even know where in London she was.

Then she saw the carriage pull out of shadows farther along the street. Jem sprang down from the box, lowered the steps, and handed her silently inside. She settled against the seat back with a sigh of relief. Somehow, she was safe and on her way home, with memories to last a lifetime. She would not, of course, risk any further meetings with Richard in the guise of Marie Antoinette.

Brampton also saw the carriage pull out of the shadows and take his angel away. The carriage was unmarked, the horses unidentifiable in the dark, the coachman masked and well covered with a dark cloak. He had gained no answers, then, from this spying on her. But she must be a member of the Quality, as he had suspected. The conveyance and horses had appeared expensive. The coachman had been prompt in meeting his lady. She had loyal followers, then. He hoped that she would not be caught and questioned by the old fool of a husband that he had her coupled with in his imagination.

Brampton lit the candles, dressed at a leisurely pace, and wandered into Devin's library in search of a brandy decanter. He felt himself honor-bound to wait out the half-hour. That time limit was not going to seem half as tedious as the week he would have to live through before seeing her and holding her again, he thought ruefully.

8

In the following week it seemed to Margaret as if her hopes for an attachment between Charlotte and Captain Charles Adair were to be realized. He visited daily, always claiming that he came to see both ladies, but he usually ended up near Charlotte, talking to her almost exclusively, while Margaret entertained any other visitors who happened to be there, or sat quietly at her embroidery if there were none. On several afternoons Charlotte was invited to drive in the park with the captain. Margaret was asked to join them too, on each occasion, but each time she felt as if she had been invited as a polite afterthought. Each time she declined.

One evening they spent at Almack's, the famous Marriage Mart, where guests danced and socialized by strict invitation only, in the form of vouchers granted by one of four patronesses. Charlotte's pretty face and figure and her bubbly personality ensured her plenty of partners. But Margaret was especially pleased to see her dance twice with Charles. It would have been improper for her to dance more times with him than that, but she sat with him during a few more dances, talking and laughing and fanning herself.

Margaret was pleased. She herself danced absent-mindedly with several of her husband's friends, and she chattered with her female acquaintances. But she was not bent on her own amusement. All her interest was pinned on her sister and her brother-in-law. And her heart was at the opposite side of the ballroom, where Brampton stood conversing with a small knot of men, looking resplendent in a tight-fitting mulberry-colored velvet coat and gray silk knee breeches, with his usual pure white linen and lace. He had escorted her in one country dance after their arrival, and then had moved on to a more congenial pastime, his duty done.

"Lady Brampton, may I have the honor?" The languid voice and the lace-covered hand belonged to Devin Northcott.

She smiled, laid her hand in his, and allowed him to lead her onto the floor. As the orchestra began to play, she realized with a feeling of disappointment that it was a waltz. She had hoped that Richard would waltz with her once. She smiled calmly up at Devin as she placed a small, gloved hand on his shoulder and followed him into the rhythm of the dance. A quick glance showed her that Brampton was still deep in conversation, his back to the dance floor. Charlotte and Charles, who was looking unexpectedly magnificent in blue satin civilian clothes, were seated together in an alcove of the large ballroom, seemingly with eyes only for each other. This was the second dance she had sat out with him. Margaret made a mental note to make sure that they were separated for the next set. It would not do to allow gossip to develop, at Almack's of all places.

"You dance very daintily, ma'am. Feel as if I had a feather in m' arms," commented Devin.

"Thank you, sir," Margaret replied, "but a woman can only be as good a dancer as her partner, you know." She smiled again as he turned her in the

dance, and caught Brampton's eye as he faced
around and lazily scanned the room.

"Is Captain Adair feeling better?" asked Devin
conversationally. "Notice he don't wear his arm in a
sling anymore."

"I believe he wore it that first night only to put his
mama's mind at rest," Margaret said with a chuckle.
"Maybe he also knew that it gave him a very
romantical look."

"Wouldn't know about that, ma'am," he said with
a cough.

"Oh, ask any of the ladies," she said airily.

"Very close family, the Adairs," said Devin. "He
spends a lot of time with Bram?"

"Not really," said Margaret. "He visits our house
every day, but Richard is usually away in the afternoons."

There was silence for a while. Margaret felt a little
uncomfortable. Devin knew that Charles spent most
afternoons with her and her sister. He had been
there himself on a few of those occasions. And he had
excused himself early, without any of his usual
invitations for Charlotte to drive out with him.
Margaret felt a little sorry for him. She did not wish
to see him hurt, but she could not really think him a
suitable partner for her very young sister.

Devin coughed again. "Really not my business,
Lady Bram," he said, forgetting for the moment that
he had never before called her by the shortened form
of her name, "but should Miss Wells be so long with
the same partner? All the same to me, but the old
tabbies can be pretty vicious, y'know."

Margaret raised her eyebrows. "Indeed, Mr.
Northcott," she said rather frostily, "I have been
observing her carefully and had planned to have her
partnered with someone else for the next set. Maybe

you would like to rescue her from the scandal that seems to be brewing."

Devin blushed rather painfully and opened his mouth to speak.

"May I claim a husband's privilege and cut in on you, Dev?" asked a pleasant and dearly familiar voice from behind Margaret, and before she knew it she had changed partners and was being twirled into the waltz by a much more confident and competent partner. Although the tempo of the dance had not changed, Margaret was having difficultly catching her breath. She fixed her eyes on the complicated folds of Brampton's neckcloth. Only once did she look up into his face, but she immediately looked down again—and momentarily stumbled—when she found his eyes fixed steadily on her, their expression quite unreadable. His hand tightened reassuringly against the small of her back. She smiled fleetingly in the general direction of his chin.

"Pardon me, Richard," she said. She was feeling a growing ball of tension building inside her. Only a few evenings before he had danced with her at Vauxhall. Surely he would recognize at any moment that he was holding the same woman.

"You will be making me jealous, my dear," he said very quietly, "if you smile so sweetly at all your dancing partners."

Margaret's eyes shot up to his. His eyes were gleaming, but she was not sure if it was with amusement or not. Before she could respond, he spoke again.

"I see that Dev is performing our duty," he said, and Margaret looked to the alcove where she had last seen Charlotte and Charles *tête-à-tête*. Now they were standing, and Devin was talking to them in his languid manner.

"We must watch the proprieties more carefully where Charlotte is concerned," Brampton said, looking back to his wife, the gleam now gone from his eyes. She had the feeling that she was being scolded, that he had really meant "*You* must watch . . ."

Brampton was not sure himself whether his words to his wife had been meant teasingly or not. He had felt unaccountably irritated a few minutes before to see her looking so happy in Northcott's arms. His hand splayed on her back had looked too intimate; her hand on his shoulder had seemed too close to his neck. Yet he had caught himself up in the thoughts with a grimace of self-mockery. Was he jealous of his little mouse of a wife?

He could not at all understand his feelings. A few nights before, when he had made such passionate love to the other woman, he had been convinced that only she meant anything in his life. He was almost prepared to cast everything he owned and everything he was over the moon in order to be with her for the rest of his life. And he still longed with all his being for the rest of the week to pass in order to see her again.

He had not visited his wife's room since that other night because, he had told himself, it would be tedious and distasteful to be with her after the other passionate encounter. But as he watched her dance and talk with Northcott, he admitted that his reason was perhaps that he felt unworthy of her. She was always so sweet, so composed, so unassuming. He realized, with something like shock, that he was missing her. He drew peace and sanity from contact with her quiet little body.

His feet carried him, without conscious will, across the ballroom to perform the not quite socially acceptable action of cutting in on another man's dance.

Brampton felt an almost disturbing surge of relief as he held his wife in a gentle hold and felt her respond to his lead in the dance. His reactions annoyed himself. He covered them by criticizing her for allowing her sister to spend a little too much of the evening with his brother. He watched a faint blush of color mount her cheeks, the only sign of emotion, as she replied calmly to his words.

"I shall make sure that Charlotte has another partner for the next set, Richard," she said.

Charlotte was up unusually early the next morning. In fact, she was dressed, had breakfasted, and was ready to leave when Captain Charles Adair called for her before noon. He had discovered the night before that she could ride, and they had arranged to ride together in the park the next morning. Jem had had a quiet mare from the stables saddled for her; the horse was waiting outside, beside Charles' black stallion.

"You look very dashing this morning, Charlotte," Charles said with a grin, holding out his hands to form a step for her foot and tossing her up into the sidesaddle.

"Thank you, kind sir," she replied jauntily, and grinned back down at him. She knew she looked well. The jonquil riding dress and daring little hat that tilted over one eye, with a curled brown feather that circled an ear, had been carefully chosen to accentuate her youthful high spirits and auburn hair. She had had the outfit made with someone else's admiration in mind, but that did not matter now. She was not going to spoil such a morning.

"You suit the morning," Charles continued

gallantly, "bright and gay. And especially bright to me. I had a letter from Juana this morning."

"Did you indeed!" Charlotte flashed him a bright smile before turning back to watch her horse's step on the street. "And does she still love you, Charles?"

"But of course," he answered, eyebrows raised. "How could she resist?"

"How, indeed," she responded. "I have observed nothing but swooning females in your wake wherever you go."

He laughed aloud. "Wretch! And how is it that you have been able to resist my fatal charm?"

"Perhaps because I have an instinct for self-preservation, sir," she replied. "When a gentleman confides in me his undying love for 'the most lovely lady in the world,' during our first conversation together, I have the common sense to know it would be unwise to develope a *tendre* for that gentleman."

He laughed again. "Charlotte, my love," he said, "I wish you were my younger sister."

"Goodness!" she responded. "Is that meant to be a compliment?"

They turned into the park and were able to relax their vigilance over the horses, which broke simultaneously into a trot.

"And what does your Juana have to say?" Charlotte asked after a few minutes of easy silence.

"She has hopes of her brother soon agreeing to her coming here to England," he said.

"Charles, that's wonderful! And you will marry her?"

"Of course!"

"Yet you have still said nothing about her to your mother or any other member of your family?"

"Juana is nobly born," Charles explained, "but her family has lost most of their possessions in the wars.

When I met her, she was living in near-poverty with her brother and his family in a five-room apartment in Madrid. Mama and Dick are very high in the instep, not to mention Rosalind and the other girls. I fear they would throw all kinds of objections in the way if I were to announce my secret betrothal. No, I still feel it better to wait until she arrives in England. I know they will not be able to resist her when they see her. Oh, Charlotte, you should see her dark hair and flashing black eyes. She flies up into the boughs at the slightest provocation." He chuckled at some private memories.

"Yes, it will be most exciting to meet her," agreed Charlotte.

"In the meantime," he continued, "Mama is pushing in my direction all the insipid and simpering misses the Season has to offer."

"Of which number I am one," Charlotte said tartly.

"You? Insipid and simpering? Never!" he said. "You have perhaps too much spirit for your own good. But I am grateful to you for agreeing to spend so much time with me. It gives me breathing space. I hope I am not keeping you away from any particular admirer. Am I, Charlotte?"

"Oh, indeed not," she assured him brightly. "I have no intention of fixing my choice yet."

He looked searchingly into her face and grinned. "It sounds as if I have touched you on the raw."

Charlotte kicked the side of the horse. "I'll race you to that large oak!" she shouted, pointing ahead about half a mile. The mare, unused to such treatment and startled out of a steady trot, broke into a sudden and panicked gallop. Charlotte leaned forward and clung to the reins. She gave herself up to a feeling of exhilaration. It seemed an age since she had last enjoyed a clandestine gallop with Meg at home.

Devin Northcott and the Earl of Brampton were riding slowly in the opposite direction, discussing the issues of a morning debate in the House.

"By Jove, it's Miss Wells!" Devin suddenly exclaimed, paling noticeably. The next moment his horse sprang into a gallop, responding to the vicious prod of Devin's spurs.

A startled Brampton took in the scene at a glance. Charlotte was indeed flying in his direction, bent low over her horse's neck. Charles was in hot pursuit, and Northcott was now approaching at an angle designed to cut her off. Brampton could not decide on the instant if Charlotte was in danger or not, but he also spurred his horse ahead.

Charlotte was suddenly made aware of another horseman—Mr. Northcott!—galloping toward her, wheeling his horse sharply about, and bringing it in close to hers. The race took on a new thrill. She felt sudden indignation, though, when his hand reached out and caught her horse's bridle just above the bit and hung grimly on until the mare slowed to a trot and then stopped altogether.

Devin dismounted quickly, grasped Charlotte firmly by the waist, and lifted her to the ground. He held her against his fast-beating heart for a few moments until he became aware of the impropriety of such a situation.

"Quite safe now, my dear," he muttered soothingly to the feather of her riding hat. "Must tell Bram to find you a quieter mount."

Charlotte, who had been furious at being so effectively prevented from completing the race, was by now unaccountably demure. "Mr. Northcott, whatever would I have done without you?" she said breathlessly.

He coughed. "Glad to be of service," he said.

"Were you really in danger, Charlotte, my love?" Charles asked with concern, dismounting beside them and breaking a certain spell.

"I have not much experience at riding," she lied meekly.

"I suggest that you take Charlotte home at once and let my wife tend to her, Charles," Brampton said from his horse's back.

Charlotte held out a timid right hand. "Thank you, sir," she said, smiling shyly up at Devin, "for saving me from a nasty tumble."

"M' pleasure," he mumbled, bowing over her hand.

"Charlotte, you fraud," was Charles' sympathetic comment as they rode away in the direction of the park entrance. "You were not in danger for one moment. That fellow has a *tendre* for you. Were you teasing him?"

"Mr. Northcott?" asked Charlotte, her eyes wide with innocence. "You mistake, sir. He is so *old!*"

He laughed. "All of thirty, I believe."

Back near the oak tree, Devin Northcott was mounting his horse again, muttering to himself. "Charlotte, my love!" he was saying in disgust.

On the following day Brampton announced that he was moving his household to the country for at least a couple of weeks. He had estate business at Brampton Court that had been needing his attention for some time. He had intended to travel down alone and stay for a few days, but had found himself making several excuses for not doing so. He and his wife had taken on the responsibility of chaperoning Charlotte during her come-out Season. Although he had every confidence in his wife's wisdom and discretion, and knew that she could control her sister's more impulsive nature, he still felt that they needed him to lend support as an escort to various social functions. He knew that he could rely on his brother and his best friend to escort the ladies in his absence, but somehow he found the thought distasteful.

Then, of course, there was his budding romance with the mysterious lady whom he could call only his angel. He hated to leave just at a time when he had established contact with her again, and just when it seemed that a very satisfactory affair was developing. But then again, he found that the situation was not really bringing him much joy. He did not want an affair with her; he wanted a relationship. And, even more confusing, there was the fact that he wanted to be faithful to his wife; he wanted to build an affectionate relationship with her, too.

Finally Brampton had to admit that his real reluctance to leave had entirely to do with his own comfort. Who, at Brampton Court, would remember to order his favorite meals? Who would listen quietly and with interest to his political theories and his various concerns over his estates, his horses, and other personal matters? And who would screen his visitors so that he saw only persons he would find interesting, while she sat patiently conversing with all the bores? Brampton did not love his wife as he loved his angel, he did not desire her as passionately, but he was beginning to find the thought of being away from her deuced uncomfortable.

There were only a few weeks of the Season left, and Brampton did not want to cut it short, for Charlotte's sake. On the other hand, some of the business he had to attend to would not wait. Brampton hit on the happy solution of organizing a house party at Brampton Court, so that his sister-in-law could have all the social activities that she could possibly want.

He summoned his wife to the library after breakfast and put the suggestion to her.

"Well, what do you think, my dear?" he asked, leaning back in the chair behind his desk and steepling his fingers as he watched her sitting quiet and straight-backed in the chair across from his. "Will you be bored in the country? Will Charlotte be disappointed to miss the vast whirl of balls and breakfasts and such?"

"I cannot speak for Charlotte, Richard," she answered earnestly, "but I should like it of all things. It is turning so hot and dusty in the city now. It will be perfectly splendid to be back at Brampton Court with its lawns and trees. And the lake," she added. She gazed eagerly across the desk at him so that he sat dazed by the life that had welled up in her.

"Do you prefer the country to the city?" he asked with curiosity.

"Yes, indeed I do, Richard," she replied. "But of course," she added, suddenly aware of her own enthusiasm and covering it for fear he would think her childish, "I am happy to be wherever you wish to be."

"Now that we have Charlotte launched," he said, gazing at her so intently that she lowered her eyes to the hands clasped in her lap, "we shall be able to spend more time at home. My father always preferred to live there, and live there we did until his death when I was sixteen. It is a good place for children."

Margaret tried to stop herself from blushing as her hands clasped together more tightly. She wondered if her husband's absence from her room since the night of Vauxhall had solely to do with what had happened that night or if he had been counting weeks and had assumed this was the time when he could not touch her. But nothing had happened in its regular cycle, and she had been living from hour to hour in painful hope.

Brampton broke into her thoughts. "Do you think we can arrange a house party at such short notice?"

"If we begin today, yes," she answered calmly. "How many guests did you have in mind, Richard?"

"About twelve?"

"And whom do you wish to invite?"

"Mother and Charles, certainly. Northcott will come, though I am sure he will stay at his own home, since it is only three miles away. Lucy and Henry have been angling for an invitation this twelvemonth or more. You may choose the others, my dear. May I suggest choosing young people who will be congenial to Charlotte?"

And that was almost the full extent of the plans that Brampton made himself. It was Margaret who, for the next week, worked almost nonstop writing invitations, sending notice of their arrival to Brampton Court, deciding what possessions were to be packed and taken and which staff members were to accompany the family, and trying to ensure that Charlotte still had a full social life.

Charlotte was quite happy with the new arrangements. Although she was a high-spirited girl, she was not silly. She was beginning to find the almost constant round of social activities rather boring. One tended to see the same faces wherever one went. One learned what compliments to expect from which gallants, what confidences to expect from which girls, and what invitations one was likely to receive from which members of the *ton*. She had her regular circle of admirers, but had found that only one of them had the power to increase her heartbeat, and he seemed to have lost interest in the last few weeks. She had been thankful for Charles' company. He was fun and easy to be with, and since everyone seemed to assume that he was a front-runner for her affections, she was not so constantly pestered by boring and languishing young men.

Charlotte helped Margaret pick out the guests for the house party. Her two close friends, Annabelle Frazer and Susanna Kemp, were to come with Susanna's amiable brother Ted; the twins, Rodney and Kenneth Langford, and Miss Faith Axton, betrothed to the latter, were invited. The dowager countess, on hearing of the party, also requested that her friends, Lord and Lady Romley, be included. All were able to come, even at such short notice.

Only one thing was allowed to take Margaret's mind off the impending house party, and that was her appointment to meet her husband again at Vauxhall. Charlotte was worried about the event, too.

"Meg, you must go," she pleaded when Margaret claimed for at least the twentieth time that week that the original plan had been rather childish and must be forgotten.

"We did not think further than the first meeting, Lottie," she explained. "There is nothing left to prove. Yes, he did find me attractive at the Hetherington ball six years ago, and yes, he does find me attractive now in the same disguise." Margaret did not explain just how attractive he was finding her. "But I cannot go on with the deception. He will find me out sooner or later. And even if he does not, what is to be gained?" Except a lot of wild, uninhibited happiness, she added silently.

"But we cannot give up now, Meg," Charlotte argued. "He loves you. But he does not know that it is you he loves. You will still insist on behaving so primly all the time. And you still wear your hair in those old-maidenly braids. You have to tell him, Meg."

"Impossible, Lottie! Such an interview would be horribly embarrassing and a terrible blow to Richard's dignity."

"Phooey!" Charlotte exploded. "Is it undignified to have a wife that loves one?"

Margaret sighed. "However," she said, chiding herself for a weakening resolve, "perhaps I should don the disguise and meet him one more time. It will surely be the last time, if we are to spend some weeks in the country."

Charlotte jumped to her feet, clapping her hands. "Oh, Meg," she said, bending over her sister and hugging her, "it will all turn out, you will see. I never knew of such a stupid situation as this, where two people love each other so much and cannot say so."

"You have so much experience," Margaret teased affectionately.

9

BRAMPTON WAITED AT the same tree as he had chosen the week before. He had feared earlier that rain would spoil the evening, but although the sky was still heavy with clouds and the air was unseasonably cool, it had remained dry. The revelers had certainly not stayed away. They passed him on the path in couples and in groups, talking quietly among themselves or noisily joking and laughing. Sounds of music floated to him from the orchestra stand just beyond the trees. Colored lanterns swayed in the breeze and made the area even more of an enchanted land.

Brampton drew his black cloak even more closely around him. She was late tonight. What if she did not come at all? Part of him felt relief—he would be released from an impossible situation. And part of him felt something very like panic. He would have no way of tracing her if she did not come. He might never see her again!

And then he spotted her, tripping lightly along the path, a gray woolen cloak drawn over the silver gown, a gay smile on her lips and in her eyes.

"*Bon soir*, monsieur," she greeted him, extending to him a gloved hand in which she clasped her closed fan. "I thought perhaps the inclement weather would keep you indoors tonight."

"Not if that would keep me away from you, angel," he responded warmly. And he gathered her to him and kissed her smiling lips. "Shall we go?" He indicated the direction in which he had left his carriage.

"No, monsieur. I wish to sample the delights of Vauxhall. The food, the dancing, the fireworks, *c'est bien*?"

"Angel," he protested, "there is more than an hour to wait until the fireworks display. We will catch our deaths of cold before then. Besides," he added, lowering his voice seductively, "I had definite plans for keeping you warm, sweet."

She tossed her head and pouted. "You told me, monsieur, that you loved me," she said. "I see that you love me for only one reason."

"Angel, that is not true," he protested, amused as usual by her theatrics. "I love you for your pertness and your zest for life—and for your ability to twist me around your little finger, you minx."

He took her little hand in his and strolled along the path with her, toward a wider avenue and brighter lights. They walked and talked, sampled the wafer-thin slices of ham for which the gardens were famous, danced, and walked more.

Brampton felt an unexpected flatness of spirits. She had not been correct in saying that he loved her for one thing only, yet there was enough truth in her accusation to make him uncomfortable. He wanted to get to know her, to take her other places and do other things with her than take her to bed to make love to her. But he felt hemmed in on every side. She was not a lightskirt. He could not set her up in a house where he could visit her and spend time with her at his leisure. If they met in public places—even here, where they were in disguise—there was always the chance that he would be recognized. Very few people would be disturbed to see him with a woman other than his wife, but he dreaded the possibility of causing her pain if rumor of his infidelity should reach her. It seemed that the only place he could take her was to the rooms of the ever-faithful Devin Northcott. And once there, it was inevitable that they should end up in bed together. Brampton could just not see any happy future for their liaison.

She seemed to read his thoughts. They were strolling again along one of the darker, quieter paths, the blowing branches above their heads making a web of shadows ahead of them. They had been silent for a time.

"It is like walking along a path with a dead end, is it not, monsieur?" she asked quietly.

"Mm?"

"It is too late for us," she said. "We must stop meeting."

He did not answer for a while. They continued to walk slowly along the path; then he turned aside and led her among the trees until they were out of sight of passersby. He gathered her into his arms and laid his cheek against her ear. She wrapped her arms around his waist, beneath his cloak. They stood thus for a long while, without exchanging a word.

Brampton finally broke the silence. "You are right, my angel," he said softly, "but how can I bear to let you go?"

"I am just a dream from your past," she said sadly. "You will forget me."

"Never," he denied fervently. "And you, angel, will you forget me?"

"I shall have to find happiness with what I have, monsieur," she replied.

"And is that possible, angel? Do you love your hus-
and?"

She hesitated. "*Oui,* monsieur," she said almost in
. whisper.

"Then why," he asked in wonder, looking down
nto her face and tracing her jawline with his finger,
have you come to me, angel?"

Again she hesitated. "He does not love me," she
aid, "and sometimes I feel the need of a man's love."

He hugged her to him again, trying to recover from
he blow of learning that she did not really love him,
ut another man who was too much of a fool to
ealize what a treasure he possessed.

"And you, monsieur," she was asking hesitantly,
do you love your wife?"

Brampton was a long time answering. Did he? He
losed his eyes and tried to picture himself holding
is wife like this. She would feel very similar—more
hy, a little stiffer, less yielding. But the size was
ight. He felt a nameless yearning that he did not
vait to explore.

"Yes," he said abruptly at last, and was not at all
ure whether he had given a truthful answer or not.
He did not notice the suddenly wildly beating heart
of his companion because he had pushed away from
er and taken her hand in his again. He led her back
o the path, feeling unutterably depressed.

"Come, angel," he said, "let us forget the fireworks
or tonight. Come with me to where we can say good-
ye in private. Will you?"

"*Oui,*" she said sadly.

The next two days were almost impossibly busy
nes for Margaret. She had all the last-minute prep-
rations to make for the departure to Brampton

Court and most of the instructions to give for the
closing up of the town house, since it was unlikely
that they would be back before the summer was
over, at the earliest. Brampton spent most of those
two days at his desk in the library looking after the
business side of the removal. Charlotte rushed about
in high spirits, helping no one, generally getting
under everyone's feet, but keeping an air of cheer
fulness in the house.

Margaret was glad to be busy. She did not want to
think about that evening with Richard until she was
in the country again, where perhaps she would be
able to steal away sometimes and think, where the
surroundings would be peaceful and soothing.
Charlotte had come to her room at eleven o'clock the
next morning, unable to contain her impatience any
longer. Margaret had still been in a sleep of exhaus-
tion, not having arrived home until four o'clock in
the morning, dangerously near to dawn, in fact.

"Meg, wake up," she had said, plumping herself
down on the edge of the bed. "Tell me everything that
happened."

"There is nothing much to tell, Lottie," Margaret
had lied. "But we shall not be meeting that way
again."

"Why ever not?"

"We both agreed that there was no point, Lottie.
We were in a dead-end situation."

"Well, but what did he *say*, Meg? Was it his
decision not to meet again?"

"No, but he agreed with me. He did say one thing,
though," Margaret had said shyly. "He said he loved
me."

"Yes, I know that, Meg. He has said so before.
What we need is a plan—"

"No, Lottie," Margaret had interrupted, "I mean that he said he loves *me*, Margaret."

Charlotte had stared, openmouthed. "Meg!" she had exclaimed. "I *knew* it would all turn out well. But why, featherbrain, did you not take that as your cue? You should have swept off your wig and your mask and said something like 'Here I am, my love,' and then you would have fallen into each other's arms and lived happily ever after."

Margaret had laughed. "You read too many romances, Lottie," she said. "Now, will you leave me while I ring for Kitty and get up?"

That was all they had said on the subject. Brampton had been very quiet for two days—very remote, almost morose. Margaret, who had been filled with such wild hopes by his words at Vauxhall, had fallen back on doubt. He was, as ever, unfailingly courteous to her, but he rarely looked at her or talked to her as he had been accustomed to do. And he had not been to her bed for more than a week.

It was in this rather tense state of affairs that the removal to Brampton Court was made. Margaret and Charlotte rode in the earl's traveling carriage and picked up the dowager before leaving the city. The luggage was piled into two coaches that followed. Kitty and Stevens also rode in one of the baggage coaches. Brampton rode his favorite bay stallion, sometimes riding alongside the carriage so that he could check on the welfare of the ladies. Margaret wished with all her heart that she could ride alongside him. It was so hot and stuffy inside the carriage.

There was to be a two-day interval between the arrival of the earl and his family group and the coming of the house guests. Margaret found, to her relief, that the staff at Brampton Court, under the

able leadership of Mrs. Foster, had all the arrange
ments so well planned that there was little to do
before the arrival of her guests. She spent the time
wandering from room to room and poring over
menus to see that no detail had been forgotten, and
wandering in the gardens, notably the rose garden,
cutting fresh blooms for the house and breathing her
fill of country air. Brampton spent most of his time
in the library, dealing with the urgent business of the
estate before his guests claimed the bulk of his time.

It was in the rose garden, on the morning of the
guests' arrival, that Margaret allowed her thoughts
to dwell on what had happened between her and her
husband a few nights before. She sat on a wrought
iron seat, breathing in the fragrance of hundreds of
roses growing around her in bushes, creeping over
the low wall that separated the flower garden from
the southern lawn, and trailing over an archway that
led to a stone fountain.

She had found that evening most painful, just as if
she really were taking a final farewell of Richard.
She realized now that she had made a terrible
mistake in following Charlotte's plan. She had led
Richard into a passionate and seemingly illicit relationship with a woman he thought to be a stranger.
She had not made him happy. He had seemed
devastated at their parting. And she had not made
herself happy. She had tasted all the delights of the
love she wished to share with her husband, but had
cut herself off from a continuance of that love.

She could not possibly tell him the truth now, tell
him the identity of his unknown lover. And it was too
late for her to try to show him that she, Margaret,
would welcome a warmer, more physical relationship with her husband. They had grown into too firm
a pattern in the months since their marriage.

Besides, she would be even more terrified than she already was that he would discover the truth.

Margaret thought of the previous two nights when Richard had resumed his visits to her bedchamber. Nothing had changed. Not a word, a look, or a gesture suggested that he had meant what he had said when he told her that he loved his wife. And those brief minutes of physical union had been almost unbearable when she had longed to wrap her arms around him, twine her legs about his, and seek the warmth of his mouth with her own.

And yet it had been sweet to know that he had come back to her! Margaret was still nursing the secret and growing hope that she was carrying her husband's child.

But Richard was unhappy! His face had had a closed and shuttered look in the last four days. She had not seen him smile in that time. Margaret remembered how reluctant he had been to let her go that night. They had gone to the same place as before. Richard had drawn the heavy curtains across the window and doused the candles without a word before unclothing her and himself and making love to her with a silent kind of desperation. There had been no tenderness involved and no real joy, only a driving need.

He had held her afterward and soothed her and whispered words of love. They had not slept. Soon he had lifted her on top of him and brought her new and unexpected delights as he taught her to straddle his broad, strong body, her knees drawn up under his arms, while he took her again. Afterward, he had eased her legs down to lie either side of his, and he cradled her against his chest. They had slept that way, still joined together.

Margaret had, in fact, come dangerously close to

being caught in the light of dawn. When they had woken up, she had tried to climb off both him and the bed, but he had turned, with her still in his arms, until she was trapped beneath him. And soon she had been a willing prisoner, giving and giving what she wished so desperately to spend her whole life giving him.

Even when she was finally dressed and groping for the door, Richard had scrambled, naked, off the bed and reached it ahead of her. He had held her in a bruising hug for several minutes, not saying a word, not attempting to kiss her. Finally, he had let her go.

Margaret felt that she would never quite forgive herself for causing him that pain. She wiped a tear from her cheek with the back of her hand.

"Here you are, my dear," Brampton's voice said from the opening in the wall behind her. "I have to visit some of the cottages down by the river to approve some repairs. I thought you might like to ride there with me. We should be back in plenty of time to greet our guests."

Margaret turned and Brampton again had that unsettling sensation of drowning fathoms deep in her eyes, which were wide with an expression he had not seen in them before.

"I should like it of all things," she said calmly, rising to her feet and accepting her husband's arm.

10

THE FIRST FEW days of the house party were filled with noisy gaiety. All the invited guests arrived that first day except Devin Northcott, who traveled to his parents' home two days later and finally joined the Brampton Court set on the following day.

The older ladies quickly established the blue salon as their domain. There they exchanged the latest *on-dits* from town, shared stories of their children and grandchildren, and did some shameless match-making.

"My dear Isabella," Lady Romley said on one such occasion, "don't you think that Susanna Kemp and your dear son Charles would make a handsome pair?"

"She has ten thousand a year," the dowager mused. "Do you think he might form an attachment, Hannah?"

"I distinctly observed him smile at her *twice* during dinner last evening," her friend reassured her.

"Ah, it would be so comfortable to have *all* my children well established," the dowager sighed, smugly aware that Lady Romley still had two daughters to be provided with husbands.

"Of course, he does seem uncommonly fond of the earl's sister-in-law," Lady Romley commented slyly.

"Charlotte? Just a silly chit! Charles has a better notion of what is due him, never fear, Hannah," the dowager replied tartly.

"Rumor had it a while ago that Devin Northcott was about to offer for her," said Lady Romley.

"Very unlikely," the dowager decided. "Devin must be immune to all the little misses of the Season after avoiding them for ten years or more past."

"She has no dowry?" quizzed the other.

"But little," the other replied. "I have considered suggesting to dear Richard that he might marry her to the vicar of St. Stephen's. It is Richard's living, you know, Hannah, and the new man needs a wife."

"Ah," Lady Romley commented, "the gel will be grateful for that. Fetching little thing!"

The younger ladies spent much of their time wandering around, trying to look pretty. They kept to their rooms most of the morning, sleeping and preparing to meet the day. In the afternoon they wandered in the gardens, took carriage rides to various parts of the estate to see the views from the hills or to have a picnic, or sat indoors to gossip—usually about one predominant topic.

"However do you tell the twins apart?" Annabelle asked Faith wide-eyed. "I should not know which one was my betrothed!" She giggled.

"But they are both so handsome," Susanna commented. "And, Lady Brampton, is it true that Captain Adair is to return to Spain soon?"

"I believe he hopes to return before winter sets in," Margaret replied.

"How romantic it would be to follow the drum as a soldier's wife," Susanna sighed.

"It would be most disagreeble and uncomfortable,

you may be sure, Susanna," Lady Lucy commented as she stitched at a sampler.

"Is Mr. Northcott to come to dinner again this evening?" Faith asked of no one in particular. "I do think he casts the other men in the shade with his elegance."

"Never say so," Annabelle objected. "Did you not note the high points of Mr. Rodney Langford's collars last evening? I know it was not Mr. Kenneth Langford, because you were holding his arm, Faith. And did you not see his striped satin waistcoat and stockings? I like to see a man in the height of fashion. Mr. Northcott is too—too—"

"Staid?" asked Charlotte helpfully.

"There, you see?" Annabelle said triumphantly. "Charlotte agrees with me."

"I did not say that," Charlotte pointed out.

The men spent most of their days out riding, or fishing, or playing billiards indoors. Their conversation was, significantly, about horses and hunting and the latest boxing mills they had witnessed, about cards and gambling and the latest bizarre bets that had been entered in the books at the clubs.

"I say," said Ted Kemp, "did you see Bill Bruiser give Hatchet Harry a leveler in the ring last week? Two minutes into the first round. Harry had pounded Bruiser like a punching bag in the stomach. Bruiser did not even bat an eyelid. Then one left hook and *bam!* Blood pouring from Harry's nose and Bruiser being carried from the ring shoulder high."

"A damned waste of time I called it," said Charles. "It took an hour to drive out to the mill and another half-hour to find a parking spot. The whole thing was over before a man had started to watch."

"Who is going to win the race to Brighton?" Rodney Langford asked.

"What race?" asked Sir Henry.

"Viscount Harley's son and old Sangster to race their curricles from London to Brighton Saturday next," Rodney explained.

"It will probably end with a couple of broken necks," Lord Romley commented.

"Sangster's favored on the odds, I hear," said Kenneth Langford.

Very little of their conversation concerned the ladies.

The evenings were a time that the whole party spent together. After dinner, when the gentlemen had rejoined the ladies after their port, there would be pianoforte music and singing, or cards, or some impromptu dancing, or merely conversation. Once there was a lively game of charades. It was during these evenings that the older ladies gathered some of their ammunition for the next day's gossip.

Lady Romley noticed that Annabelle and Ted sat together at the pianoforte singing quietly together long after everyone else's attention had moved on to other matters. She noticed that Faith and Kenneth did not speak to each other for the whole of one evening. She noticed that Charlotte rarely talked to Devin Northcott, but that she followed him everywhere with her eyes. And she noticed the Devin spent most of his evenings talking with Lady Brampton.

The dowager Countess of Brampton noticed that Susanna tried in many ways to fix her interest with Charles. She noticed that her daughter-in-law looked tired. She definitely had the look of one who was *enceinte*, she confided in an undertone to her friend the next day ("so wonderful for dear Richard to have an heir at last, Hannah"). She noticed Charlotte disappear through the French windows one evening with Charles while most of the others were at cards. And she noticed them returning more than half an hour later.

"Charlotte, my love, do you wish to rescue a drowning man?" Charles had said. "Come and walk in the garden with me."

"What, does Susanna Kemp not compare with your Juana?" Charlotte asked cheekily when they were outside. She tucked her arm comfortably through his.

"Have you heard of the difference between night and day, brat?" he asked.

"You really are being most cruel to all the ladies, you know, Charles," she scolded gaily. "Here they all are, falling over themselves trying to ensnare you, and you will not even warn them that you are betrothed."

"Should I wear a sign?" he asked. "And can I help it, my love, if I was born with quite irresistible charm?"

"And with incredible immodesty," Charlotte commented to the stars.

They went to sit on the stone wall surrounding the fountain in the rose garden.

"Juana is really coming to England," Charles announced.

"Oh? When?" Charlotte clapped her hands.

"She was not sure of that. The war had disrupted life in Spain. It may be weeks or only days before she arrives in Portsmouth. She may even now be on the seas. She is to send me a message when she arrives. I can be there from here in four hours or less."

"Charles, do you not think it would be wise to tell your mama or his lordship that she is coming?"

"No, I do not," he answered. "It will be time enough for them to know when she is here. They cannot possibly see her and not fall in love with her on the instant."

Charlotte could not help but feel that he was looking at the situation through a lover's eyes, but she kept her counsel.

Lord Romley one evening showed interest in the old Norman church at Brampton town, four miles away.

"Yes, it is in very good repair," the earl replied to a question directed at him, "and almost entirely original. It is still used as our parish church."

"The new vicar is very knowledgeable about it," Margaret added. "He knows every tomb and the history of everyone buried there."

"We will be going there to church next Sunday," Brampton added, "but in the meanwhile, we could arrange an excursion there if anyone is interested."

"Splendid!" said Faith. "Do you not agree, Kenneth?"

It seemed that everyone agreed. The excursion was set for the following afternoon, weather permitting. Meanwhile, the evening's conversation became brisk with plans for conveying sixteen people—Devin Northcott said he would ride over to the house after luncheon and make one of the party. It was decided that the closed traveling carriage and the open landau would together convey twelve people. Devin offered to take one other person up with him in his curricle. Two of the men would ride.

The following afternoon proved perfect for an outing. The sun shone from a cloudless sky; there was no wind to threaten hats or bonnets or carefully placed curls of hair. The ladies, bright and summery in their silks and sprigged-muslin dresses, were able to dispense with shawls and pelisses, but not with their parasols.

Lady Romley and the dowager Countess of Brampton were helped into the closed carriage. The dowager declared that although the day was hot and still now, a treacherous breeze would be caused by the movement of the carriages and might bring chills with it. Better to be safe inside a closed conveyance, she said. They were joined by Lucy and Sir Henry, Faith and Kenneth.

Annabelle and Ted climbed into the landau and sat side by side, facing the horses. Charles had that morning offered to take his curricle, on the private condition that Charlotte ride with him.

"I shall leave the landau for Lady Brampton," Susanna now announced loudly and magnanimously, "that is, if Captain Adair will not object to my company in his curricle?" She fluttered her eyelashes in his direction.

What could he do? He gave the expected gallant reply, grasped her plump waist, and hoisted her into the high seat beside his. He threw a helpless glance in Charlotte's direction.

Lord Romley and Rodney Langford meanwhile appeared on horseback, ready to accompany the carriages.

Devin Northcott was quick to size up the remaining possibilities. He did not wish to place Miss Wells in an embarrassing situation.

"Lady Brampton," he said smiling and extending a hand to her, "d'ye trust my driving well enough to accompany me? Am considered an adequate whip. Ask Bram there."

Margaret smiled and took his hand. "I do not need to ask, sir," she assured him. "I know I can trust such a good friend of my husband's." She allowed him to lift her carefully to her seat.

It cannot be said that either Brampton or Charlotte was entirely pleased with the turn of events, but they both conversed brightly with the two other occupants of the landau during the four-mile drive.

The vicar did indeed prove knowledgeable about the old church. He was delighted with his large and distinguished audience. He discoursed eloquently on the history and architecture of the building as he led the party down the nave toward the altar.

It soon became apparent, though, that the desire for an outing more than an eagerness for a history lesson had prompted most of the party to come. By the time the vicar reached the altar, more than half an hour after he had begun his guided tour, only Lord Romley, Margaret, Devin, Susanna, and Rodney remained of the original sixteen. Susanna would have been gone too if she had seen Charles slip away. As it was, she had to make the most of Rodney's company, commenting at one point, sotto voce, that these old buildings were frightfully cold; she shivered delicately. Rodney rejected his first instinct, which was to take off his coat and place it around her pretty, plump shoulders, and his second instinct, which was to put an arm around her; he took the only other possible course. Soon they too were headed up the aisle, her arm in his, headed for the warmth of the sun in the graveyard.

"If we stay here, Mr. Langford," she pouted prettily, "we shall be caught again by the vicar and forced to listen to the history of every horrid tombstone."

He grinned in appreciation of her opinion. "By all means, let us explore the village," he said.

Charles and Charlotte, meanwhile, were already in the village, sitting on a rustic bench outside the alehouse. They were arguing.

"I cannot ride back with you," Charlotte was explaining crossly. "It would be uncommon rude to Susanna."

"Charlotte, my love, have mercy on a man's tender constitution," Charles pleaded. "Boredom is a terrible-enough disease; it could be fatal. I might forget to continue living. But much worse is the very real danger of contracting pneumonia."

"You had better explain yourself," Charlotte said tartly. "You cannot expect silly, simpering misses to understand such obscure talk."

"By Jove, you are as cross as a bear today, are you not, my love?" Charles commented. "I merely meant that such a draft is caused by the fluttering of Miss Kemp's eyelashes that I am in mortal danger of catching a chill."

"Hmm," said Charlotte.

Charles leaned forward and looked into her face. "Out with it, Charlotte, my love," he said.

"Out with what?"

"With whatever it is that is bothering you."

"Whatever do you mean?" she said irritably. "There is nothing bothering me."

"I know you better than to believe that," he said. He thought for a while, still staring into her face. "Is this house party not to your liking?" he asked. "Is there someone missing that you would wish to be here?"

"No, of course not!"

"Hmm. Then, is there someone here that is not paying you the attention that you would wish?"

"Charles, stop this, this instant. I should like some lemonade, please."

"All in good time, my love. Who could it be? Ted Kemp? No, too milk and water for you. Rodney Langford? No, you would never be sure the right twin was making love to you. Devin Northcott? No, he is too old and set in his ways."

"He is not old," snapped Charlotte. "You told me yourself that he is but thirty."

"Aha! My love, I hope you never take to lying," he said smugly. "You would never convince anybody."

"Whatever do you mean?" she said.

"So the independent little Miss Wells is in love with a confirmed, *old* bachelor, is she?"

Charlotte opened her mouth to protest the description of Devin, then shut it again. "But I am just making a cake of myself," she said, the bad temper gone from her voice. "He does not know I exist."

"I would not say that," Charles mused. "He seemed very aware of your existence that day he rescued you from certain death in the park."

"Don't tease, Charles. This is no joke to me."

"Poor Charlotte," he commented, an affectionate smile in his eyes. "What can we do?"

"I don't know," she replied seriously. "We need a plan."

"Well, while you are devising one, smile and look cheerful," he advised. "Here comes the gentleman with your sister, and you do not wish him to know that you are languishing for him, do you?"

Charlotte smiled.

The vicar had finally exhausted all the information he knew about the interior of the church. He suggested that he take his party of three into the graveyard to show them some of the older and more interesting tombstones.

Margaret lagged behind as they emerged from the

cold darkness of the stone building into the bright heat out of doors.

"Take m' arm, Lady Bram?" Devin offered, turning back to her and perceiving her fatigue.

"Thank you, Mr. Northcott, but I must find somewhere to sit down for a while," Margaret replied. "I have become dizzy from so much standing."

"Lean on me, ma'am," he said, looking into her face with concern.

While the vicar disappeared around the eastern corner of the church with the one remaining member of his audience, Devin led Margaret to sit on the low stone wall surrounding the churchyard.

"Ah, that is better. Thank you," said Margaret, sighing.

"Not feeling quite the thing, Lady Bram?"

"Oh, I shall be fine now," she said. "If it were just not so hot!"

"Shall I fetch Bram to you, ma'am?"

"Oh, no," Margaret said hastily. "Really, sir, I shall be quite rested in a few minutes."

"May I?" he asked, and sat beside her on the wall when she nodded. He removed a handkerchief from the pocket of his waistcoat and used it, without too much effect, to fan her face beneath the brim of her chipstraw bonnet.

Margaret, whose feeling of faintness and slight nausea was leaving her, suddenly saw the humor of the scene. She turned and laughed up into his face, bare inches away. "Thank you, Mr. Northcott," she said gaily. "I feel quite recovered now, but I think your handkerchief was meant for other uses, sir."

Neither of them noticed the party of four which had just emerged from a confectioner's shop across the street. Devin helped Margaret to her feet, took her arm, and led her toward the tavern, where he hoped to find some shade and some water or lemonade for her.

Lord Brampton escorted Susanna and Annabelle into a haberdasher's store, but he took no part in the discussion they were having with Rodney Langford about the choice of some ribbons. He was brooding on the radiant smile his wife had just bestowed on his best friend, and at such close quarters.

11

NOBODY WAS EVER quite sure where the idea for the Brampton Court Fair originated. All the house guests seemed to contribute some idea. It began perhaps with Margaret's suggestion to her husband that they give a large dinner party for all the leading families of the area. Someone—perhaps Brampton himself, perhaps Charles—added the idea that perhaps, since they were going to all the trouble of inviting and catering to so many people—eight families in addition to the house guests, they might as well have a ball too.

Someone else—Charlotte perhaps?—thought it a shame that only the wealthier families should be part of the festivities. Yet how could one invite all the tenants to dine at the house? Soon there was a tumult of suggestions, most of which centered around the idea of moving the activities out of doors.

Eventually some sort of ordered plan emerged. The festivities were to include all the tenants of the estate and their children, and the invited families of the neighborhood. And they were to begin during the afternoon. There were to be races, pony rides, and other games for the children, baking and needlework competitions for the women, games of skill and strength for the men. There were to be booths for drinks and other refreshments.

During the early evening, oxen and pigs were to be roasted on outdoor spits for the tenants to feast on while the invited guests dined in the house. In the evening there was to be a dance out on the flat, lower lawn before the house. It was to be an occasion at which the rich would rub shoulders with the poor.

Invitations were sent out, the house party was extended a few days beyond the two weeks—only Sir Henry and Lady Lucy would have to return to London before the big day—and the plans were put into effect with feverish energy by the earl and the countess.

Margaret was more grateful than ever to have such a competent housekeeper as Mrs. Foster. Without any indication that she had been given an unusual assignment, that good lady began to organize the preparation of the food. It was a prodigious task, as all the tenants were to be fed liberally throughout the afternoon and evening, in addition to the regular meals for the guests and inhabitants of the house and the banquet for close to forty people.

Brampton made all the financial arrangements and made all the plans for the afternoon fair and the setting up of a large board floor on the lawn for the dancers. He arranged for the hiring of extra staff and of an orchestra.

The guests found new enthusiasm in helping with the preparations. The Langford twins accompanied Faith and Susanna into the village to choose prizes for the various competitions. Charlotte and Charles undertook to organize the children's games. The dowager and Lady Romley agreed to see that enough lamps and lanterns were gathered to hang in the trees surrounding the lower lawn. Lord Romley was seen to confer with the butler on the ordering of wines. Annabelle promised to help Margaret with flower arrangements on the day.

Margaret found her time very full with duties and obligations. She was finding herself almost constantly tired. She both welcomed and resented her lack of leisure time. She welcomed the fact that she had little time to brood on her troubles. Yet she resented the fact that she could not find the time to sit quietly and think about her situation.

Nothing had changed with Richard, except that she saw less of him than ever. Almost the only times she ever saw him alone were in the library when they were going over together some plans for the fair, and for the ten minutes or so when he visited her room each night. And on those occasions he rarely said more than a good night as he was leaving. Only on one occasion had he stayed longer or said more.

He had been later than usual coming to her, and Margaret had been dozing, curled on her side, one hand beneath her cheek. She had opened her eyes when he sat on the edge of the bed and took one of her braids in his hand.

"I am sorry, Richard," she had said, turning on to her back. "I must have fallen asleep."

He had looked down at her, his eyes smiling, but not his mouth. "My poor dear," he had said, "this is a very tiring time for you, is it not?"

"Indeed, Richard, I enjoy all the activity," she had assured him.

"But you are pale, my dear, and I noticed tonight that you played with the food on your plate instead of eating it."

"Indeed I ate sufficient, Richard," she had protested.

"And I am a cruel and selfish husband to come

demanding more of your energy when you only wish to sleep," he had teased gently, a strange twist to his mouth.

"No, Richard," Margaret had said, calling all her training to her aid to keep her voice calm and her face expressionless. Her hands beneath the bed-clothes had been clenched into tight fists. "I am your wife. I am never too tired for you."

"Then do your duty and obey this command," he had said. "Sleep, my dear." He had continued to gaze smilingly into her face, unaware of the painfully beating heart beneath the bedcovers. He had lifted the heavy braid that he was still holding, and placed it against his lips. And his lips had finally smiled.

Margaret could not obey his command. After he had left, she had wept into her pillow until she had finally gained comfort from holding the braid he had kissed against her own mouth. She had fallen eventually into an exhausted sleep.

No matter how busy her mind or her body might be over other matters, Margaret was almost con-stantly aware of her now-sure pregnancy. She felt well. Her tiredness was the only discomfort. The thought of having Richard's child growing inside her filled Margaret with a secret ecstasy that almost choked her at times. No matter what happened, or did not happen, between them in the future, part of him belonged to her and would continue to do so. Surely he would demonstrate her love when he knew, she sometimes thought. And she hoped fiercely that the child would be a boy so that Richard would be pleased with her.

Then at other times she would remember that he had married her only so that she would breed his children. Why should he love her for merely doing the duty for which she had been chosen? And would he stop coming to her altogether once he knew that his visits were no longer necessary? The thought filled Margaret with cold terror. She decided that she would wait until she was more certain before telling her husband.

For his part, Brampton did not welcome quite so eagerly the demands on his time and energy. He had arrived at the Brampton Court desperate with unhappiness over the loss of his angel and almost cursing his fate that had held her from him until it was too late for them to let their love grow openly. He had found it difficult to accept his wife's quiet, uncomplaining presence in his life. He had kept his distance from her, in an effort not to inflict his own unhappiness and ill-humor on her. For a few days he had been wretched with self-reproach. How could he have let her go without at least acquiring enough information to allow him to contact her again if he wanted? Only in his saner moments did he admit that what had happened was inevitable. There was no other alternative.

He had come into the country with the determined resolution to put the past behind him and to make a new start on his marriage. He intended to spend more time with his wife, to get to know her better, to resume his physical relationship with her.

He had found that matters were turning out not quite as planned. The obligation to entertain his guests proved quite arduous, particularly after plans for the fair got under way. He saw his wife probably more frequently than he had during the rest of their married life, but he was almost never alone with her, except when the press of business made personal talk impossible.

At night he saw her, but he always made his visits

as short as possible. It had not escaped his attention that she sometimes looked pale and tired. And he believed that her slight little figure was even thinner than it had been. He hoped that his suggested house party was not going to reduce her stamina to the point at which she would become ill.

Brampton also found that putting the past behind him and trying to work on his marriage was not as difficult as he had expected. Physically, he missed his angel terribly, but apart from that, he found there was not a great deal to miss. She had had a vitality and an impudence that had brightened his own mood, but really he had known almost nothing about her, not even her name. When he turned his attention to his wife, he discovered that she had great depth and strength of character. She was never a leading light among the people gathered at Brampton Court; one rarely heard her voice or noticed her—not unless one were deliberately watching. But Brampton began to notice that she was, in fact, a perfect hostess. She could initiate a conversation with just the right remark or question to set her companion talking on a favorite theme. Then she would sit and listen with a look of real interest.

He noticed that she quietly and unobtrusively ensured that everyone was always occupied in a way that would bring greatest satisfaction. And although Mrs. Foster was an efficient and able housekeeper, he noticed that it was his wife who really ran the household. And amazingly none of the servants seemed to resent the fact. In fact, Brampton noticed with fascination, they seemed to have a deep respect, even affection, for his wife.

Before many days had passed in the country, Brampton discovered that his wife was just the kind of person he would have liked his angel to be if he had had the chance to get to know her. Now if only his wife could have the life and passion of the other woman . . . He found himself wondering somewhat wistfully if she would allow herself to be loved, if he took the courtship very slowly and very gently.

But, he asked himself, did he want to love her? Was he ready to make the total commitment? He could not answer his own question with any satisfaction.

But he did know one thing: he was annoyed and—yes!—jealous of the friendship between his wife and Devin Northcott. He could not and did not suspect either of them of improper feelings for the other, but he resented the fact that they seemed to find it easy to converse with each other and to smile and laugh together.

Now he was concerned about his wife. She was not quite well, and he feared that this infernal fair would tax her strength beyond its limits. He found himself hoping, for the first time since his marriage, that he would not get her with child too soon. He feared that her tiny frame would make childbearing difficult for her.

The weather had turned cold and showery four days before the fair, so that everyone feared that the day was going to be ruined. However, the final preparations were put into effect the day before. Numerous booths were erected by the male servants and tenants on the lawns and in the closest meadow to the house. The women were busy at home baking or putting final stitches to the entries for the competitions next day. The wooden dancing floor was laid in place and stands erected for the orchestra. In the stables the grooms were giving unaccustomed attention to the two ponies to be used for the children's rides—brushing their coats and laying out ribbons to twine in their manes the next morning.

In the house the cook was threatening every half-hour to hand in her notice as she rushed through the endless lists of foods to be prepared and cooked. Yet during the afternoon, when the earl's chef arrived from London to help with the preparations, the threats continued for a different reason. Did his lordship think she was incapable of handling such an event on her own, without calling in "that man" who gave himself airs just because he was from the city?

Upstairs, the servants were busy, dusting, polishing, and rearranging for those guests who would be using the house. The house guests helped out where they could.

Much to everyone's delight and relief, the day itself dawned bright and cloudless. It promised to be a scorching day. Soon after noon, the earl's tenants began to gather below the house, all dressed in their Sunday clothes, all in holiday mood. One refreshment stand was already loaded with a tempting array of fruit drinks, tarts, cakes, and fudges; another with cold meat, fish pies, pasties, and other savory delicacies. The empty booths were soon covered with the exhibits of baking and needlecrafts that the women had entered for competition.

Soon the area before the house was bright with the colors of everyone's holiday clothes, loud with the talk and laughter of the adults, the cries and shrieks of the children. The house guests mingled gaily, watching the races and competitions, admiring the delicate needlework and the delicious-looking baked products on display.

Charlotte and Charles had assumed charge of the children's games. They had an audience of several fond parents, and—inexplicably—Devin Northcott. Nobody had ever suspected that he was fond of children. He looked as if he had just stepped off Bond Street, with his coat of blue superfine, his biscuit-colored pantaloons, and gleaming Hessians; and he looked bored; but he was there, watching the little tykes run and jump and laugh and scream.

Charles had worked himself into a mood of high-spirited mischief. A three-legged race was next on the agenda, he noticed. He called together all the children and Charlotte divided them into pairs, roughly according to size. Charles began to explain to them how to run the race and how to work together with one's partner in order not to trip one another. He made the explanation deliberately vague and confused.

"Look, kiddies," he said finally while they all gazed worshipfully at his tall, handsome form, "you have to see this done to know how to do it. I could show you with Miss Wells here, but I am too tall—or she is too short, whichever way you want to look at it. Now, let me see . . ." He rubbed his chin reflectively with his hand and let his eyes rove shrewdly over the small crowd of adults. "Ah, yes, of course," he said, grinning, and apparently struck with an inspiration, "Mr. Northcott is just the man we need."

"Charles!" Charlotte hissed, feeling a distinct premonition of disaster. "What—"

"Mr. Northcott," Charles continued smoothly, completely ignoring his companion, "would you oblige us by demonstrating the three-legged race with Miss Wells here?"

"Charles!"

"Yes, yes, Mr. Northcott," chorused several children's voices, and they all began clapping and cheering.

"Nasty little devils," reflected Devin without moving a facial muscle.

"Charles, are you mad?" Charlotte flared in a furious whisper. "It would not be at all proper."

"The lady is concerned with the proprieties," yelled Charles to the most cooperative part of his audience. "Do we want to see Miss Wells and Mr. Northcott demonstrate this race, kiddies?"

"Yes!" they all shrieked, right on cue.

Over their heads, Charlotte, her face hot and dismayed, met the cool, amused eyes of Devin. He had the unspeakable effrontery to wink!

"Very well," said Charlotte with angry defiance. "Mr. Northcott?"

He strolled forward. "Miss Wells, d'ye mind if I take off my coat?" he asked, all London politeness again.

"Not at all, sir," she replied crossly. "Please do not mind me."

And then her breath caught in her throat as he stripped off the coat and stood in his crisp white shirt. He was not a tall man, but he had a very masculine physique, she thought, before he turned his back to her. She admired his broad shoulders and the body that tapered to narrow waist and hips. She did not hear what Devin said to Charles as he handed over his coat.

"You've embarrassed the lady, Adair," he said coldly, one eyebrow raised disdainfully. "Bad *ton*, d'ye know?"

One difficulty was discovered as soon as Charlotte and Devin stood side by side and Charles approached them to tie a scarf around their legs. The scarf would have to be tied around their ankles as it was quite unthinkable for anyone to reach higher up Charlotte's leg than that.

Charlotte thought that she had never been so embarrassed as she felt when the scarf pulled her leg firmly against the hard surface of Devin's Hessian. But when Charles stepped back, she realized there was far worse to come.

"Used to do this all th' time with m' brothers and sisters," Devin explained, hoping to relax her by being matter-of-fact about the whole thing. "We have a better chance of not falling if we hold on to one another. Put your arm around m' waist." He put his own arm around her shoulders and gripped her upper arm.

Charlotte, utterly mortified, placed her arm around his waist and clung to a fistful of shirt, fearful that her hand might slip lower if she did not grip on to something.

"Now watch, kiddies," Charles' voice was cheerfully saying. "They are going to run to the white post and back again. Watch and see how easy it is."

"I'll count 'one, two," Devin was explaining to Charlotte. "Move the bound leg first. Ready?"

"I suppose so."

"Right. Here we go, then. 'One, two; one, two.' "

To the ecstatic cheering of the children, they moved down the meadow to the white post. Charlotte was shrinkingly aware of the heat and movement of Devin's body against her own. She had never encountered anything like such close proximity to a man before. She was terrified that she was about to be utterly missish and faint.

"Careful on the turn," Devin warned as they approached the white post.

Charlotte had a fleeting glimpse of jumping, cheering children as they rounded the post, and then she lost her stride. Devin pulled her toward him in an effort to recover their balance, and then toppled sideways—taking her with him, of course. She was conscious of sprawling over his hip; her head came to rest across his neck, her mouth against the bare skin of his throat above his neckcloth. She pushed in panic against his chest, but without much effect; her body was angled downward.

Devin quickly and firmly lifted her off his body and set her down on the grass beside him. He propped himself on one elbow and looked down at her.

"Are you hurt, Miss Wells?" he asked in concern.

"N-no, sir," she stammered, and swallowed nervously.

They both reached for something else to say and found nothing. They gaped foolishly, both suddenly aware of electricity in the air between them. Devin lifted his hand and opened his mouth. The hand seemed destined to find its way to her cheek; his mouth was about to utter heaven knows what sentiment. Neither achieved its goal.

"I never saw anything so funny since Colonel Brody's horse tossed him into a mud puddle just as he was lecturing our regiment on careless horsemanship," said Charles' voice before he broke off to roar with laughter. "The little kiddies are cracking up back there. You have made their day."

He knelt beside the hapless pair and untied the scarf that still bound them together at the ankle. Devin got to his feet and brushed himself off hastily. As he turned to help Charlotte up, he realized that he had been forestalled.

"Come on, Charlotte, my love," Charles said, still grinning, and grasping both her hands with his, he pulled her to her feet and straight into his arms.

"Poor little love," he said cheerfully, "are you all right?"

"Yes, thank you, Charles," she replied weakly into his shirt front. Devin stalked off at that point in the direction of his abandoned coat and the still-mirthful little devils, so did not hear the rest of her words. "But please remind me to give you a gentle push next time we are close to a duck pond, will you? You horrid man. How could you!"

"Well, you were talking about having to think of a plan," he said. "I was merely trying to lend a helping hand, my love. Trying to help tie the knot, and all that—pun intentional!"

"In future you can keep your hands to yourself, Captain Adair," she said haughtily. "Now, shall we get this race started?"

In the late afternoon, the dowager Countess of Brampton and Lady Romley judged the needlecraft and baking entries. Margaret presented the prizes from a dais especially erected for the occasion. Brampton himself presented the prizes to the men for the winners of the various contests of skill and strength. The dowager gave prizes to those children who were brave enough to mount the platform for them.

As the hot sun began to dip in the west, the men who had been chosen for the task lit a large bonfire in the far corner of the meadow and prepared to roast their evening meal. Gaily shouting children rushed into the nearby trees to gather more dry wood for the fire, and some lads and girls, hand in hand, followed them, only halfheartedly contributing to the growing pile of firewood.

In the meantime the people from the house had retired to their rooms to begin the long and serious task of cleaning up and getting ready for the evening banquet.

Charlotte, in her room, was still feeling mortified at the afternoon's encounter with Devin Northcott. Since realizing that she was in love with him, she had been very conscious of the age difference between them. Had he lost interest in her because she was a silly, green girl? He *had* been interested at the start, she felt sure. She had been determined to behave in a more sober and sophisticated manner when in his presence. She hoped to convince him that she could match his thirty years in behavior, even though she was in fact only eighteen.

And now look what had happened! He had seen her yelling and jumping and romping with a host of children, and he had seen her agree to an unseemly race with a gentleman, manacled by the ankle, and clinging to his shirt, just above the waistband, just like a hoyden! And falling all over him and getting her mouth soldered to his neck. It was all too humiliating to think of.

Charlotte marched over to the bellpull in her room and rang to demand of Kitty where her bathwater was. Normally she would not have been so rag-mannered, knowing as she did that the servants must be rushed off their feet with so much to do within the next couple of hours.

She paced her room, trying to block from her mind the shameful knowledge that she was *glad* they had fallen over. She would not for the world have missed that sensation of being pressed against Devin's hard male body and the warmth of his throat. What had he been about to do when that infernal Charles Adair had come along cackling with hysterical amusement? Kiss her? Declare his un-

dying love for her? Propose to her? Brush a smut
of dirt off her nose?

She shook herself with exasperation. Tonight, at
any rate, she was going to be all demure femininity.
She glanced anxiously at the gown laid out on the
bed—a lemon-yellow satin underdress overlaid with
white lace, golden ribbons to tie beneath her breasts
and to thread through her auburn curls. Very pretty
and very maidenly! She was going to look like
someone just out of the schoolroom again, certainly
not someone to attract the worldly and almost *old*
Mr. Northcott!

Kitty and two other maids arrived with the bathwater just in time to save Charlotte's sanity.

12

AFTER THE LARGE banquet was over and the men, who had lingered over their port and cigars, had rejoined the ladies in the drawing room, the whole party decided that it was time to move out of doors. A dance that was to take place in the open air and that involved the mingling of upper and lower classes was novelty enough to arouse a great deal of excitement.

Darkness had fallen, and the grounds before the house were transformed. The trees at either side of the lawns were strung with hundreds of lanterns. Poles had been set around the huge dancing floor. Each had been wreathed with leaves and flowers, and more lanterns, all a deep rose pink. Similar lamps had been set around the orchestra stand.

Long tables covered with crisp white cloths had been set on the upper lawn and were laden with refreshments of all kinds. Liveried footmen stood close to the tables to help any guests who needed assistance and to replenish any platters or bowls that were emptying too fast.

Lord Brampton held out his arm formally to escort his wife from the house. She placed a white-gloved hand on his arm. His eyes appreciated her careful appearance. She wore a rose-pink silk gown, deceptively simple. The ribbons that fell from below her breasts almost to the hemline, and the rosebuds that

158

vere entwined in the knot were of a paler pink, and
rosebuds of the same shade had been embroidered
around the scalloped hem. Margaret had been very
tempted to give in to Kitty's coaxings and allow her
hair to be dressed more becomingly. But at the last
moment she had lost her courage, and still wore the
usual braids coiled at the back of her head, though
she had allowed Kitty to push the stems of two rosebuds into the coils.

"You are looking very lovely, my dear," Brampton
commented softly close to her ear.

"Thank you, Richard," she said calmly.

The tenants of the estate clustered on the lower
lawn, close to the dance floor, watching eagerly the
rare spectacle of a large gathering of the upper
classes in all their evening finery. They set up an
impromptu cheer as the earl and countess
approached, leading the way.

Brampton signaled the orchestra and the dancing
began. He led Margaret onto the floor to begin the
first country dance. The musicians had been
instructed to play far more country dances than was
usual at a ball, so that everyone would have a chance
to know the steps. Soon the floor was crowded with
dancers making up sets, simple starched country
gowns jostling the finest satins and lace.

Charles danced the first set with Charlotte, then
danced in turn with each of the ladies of the house
party and of the other invited families. He was desperately avoiding the clutches of Susanna Kemp.
Annabelle, meanwhile, was dancing more frequently
with Ted Kemp than would have been allowed at a
formal London ball. She might have been surprised
had she known that the male house guests had a bet
on as to how soon a betrothal announcement would
be made.

Charlotte was in a determinedly gay mood. As usual, she did not lack for partners. She danced every dance, including one with Devin Northcott. It was a country dance; inevitably they were separated frequently by the various movements of the dance. It was most frustrating. There seemed to be as little chance for conversation as there had been that afternoon, when they had been lying side by side on the grass.

"You are looking particularly delightful this evening, Miss Wells," he said as the music first struck up.

"Thank you, sir," she replied. "You are very kind."

And the dance steps forced them to move off in different directions.

"Your sister and brother-in-law have excelled themselves today," he commented the next time they were together. "This is a magnificent gala."

"Yes, is it not?" she replied brightly.

And again they were headed in opposite directions. And so it continued. It was not a situation conducive of the growth of a courtship.

Charlotte waited with barely concealed impatience for a waltz. Finally the musicians began to play one. She looked quite brazenly across the floor to where Devin was conversing with the town doctor and his wife. He turned in her direction and began to move away from his companions. Her heartbeat accelerated.

"Miss Wells, I have been waiting for a waltz so that I might ask you for the honor," announced a smiling Rodney Langford, stepping into her line of vision.

She turned on him a bright smile. "How delightful!" she lied. "It would be my pleasure, sir."

She watched with chagrin over her partner's shoulder as Devin waltzed by with Meg in his arms.

At least she was glad it was Meg, rather than some simpering miss who would be batting her eyelids at him. Charlotte could have screamed as she smiled affably and chatted gaily to the unsuspecting Rodney.

Brampton was also watching his wife and Devin circle the floor, his feelings very similar to those of Charlotte. He had given the instructions for mostly country dances, yet he had insisted on a few waltzes. And he had had his wife very much in mind when he had given those orders. He wanted to make this evening a very special one for him and her. Tonight, against this unusual and magical setting, he hoped to begin wooing her love. And he had very much wanted that first waltz. He let his eyes stray along the edge of the dancing floor until they lit on the plump and pasty daughter of Sir Leonard Petrie, a fairly distant neighbor. A few moments later he was bowing gracefully over her hand and leading her into the dance.

Devin succeeded in securing the next waltz with Charlotte by the simple expedient of reserving it with her ahead of time. He held her formally, almost at arm's length. She danced with eyes lowered, quite unlike the vivacious and friendly Charlotte he had known before Bram's infernal brother had returned from the wars. Was she embarrassed, or was she just uninterested, dreaming of the younger, dashing soldier?

He inclined his head in the direction of Bram, who danced by holding his wife rather indecently close. Neither of them appeared to notice either him or his partner. Were matters improving in that strange relationship? He hoped so. He liked the sweet little countess and he certainly did not like to think of her running around London in disguise, without proper

escort. Nor did he like to think of her in his own bed
with Bram, like a common lightskirt.

Devin had made several unsuccessful attempts to
initiate a conversation with Charlotte. Desperate,
and knowing that the dance would soon end, he
suggested that they take a walk—"to get away from
this dreadful squeeze for a little while." He was
almost surprised when Charlotte agreed without
argument.

Her heart, in fact, was thumping so painfully that
she was having a hard time catching her breath. She
had been so anxious to catch his attention tonight,
yet she had found herself stupidly tongue-tied
whenever he had tried to draw her into conversation.
Perhaps she would find it easier if they strolled away
from the crowds. She placed her hand through
Devin's arm and felt safe and protected.

Devin had known Brampton Court since childhood, almost as well as he knew his father's estate.
He knew where there was a path through those
nearby trees leading to the lake half a mile distant.
And he knew that a little way into the trees was a
small lily pond, with a rustic bench close by. Given
the picturesque setting and the moonlight and the
glow from the lanterns, which would extend that far,
he felt that he had a good chance to find out if
Charlotte's affections could be reclaimed from
Charles Adair.

Charlotte also knew about the lily pond and the
bench; she had been at the court for a few weeks. She
also knew that it was not proper to go walking with a
man unchaperoned in such a place. But it was a night
when many of the rules seemed to have been relaxed.
She allowed herself to be led.

They walked among the trees and immediately
entered a different world. Lantern light and starlight

vere filtered darkly through the high branches; the
ounds of music, voices, and laughter, though not
ɔlocked out, were muted. Everywhere was the smell
ɔf wood and leaves.

Devin held his arm close to his side, Charlotte's
rapped beneath it. They became more and more
ιware of each other, their soft footsteps and the faint
rustle of her gown the only nearby sounds. By
ιnspoken consent, neither of them said a word. The
ɔond was not far into the trees. Devin would not have
ɔeen so indiscreet as to lead her far from the
:ompany.

When they reached the small clearing, Charlotte
Ietached her arm from Devin's and sat down on the
ɔench. He seated himself beside her and took her
ιand in his. They sat so for a few minutes.

"Miss Wells—Charlotte, did I embarrass you this
ιfternoon?" he asked finally, breaking the silence
vith an abrupt and nervous voice.

"In the race?" she asked, raising her eyes to him.
'That was not your fault, sir. It was just Charles
ɔeing mischievous."

"Would not for the world cause you pain," he said,
ιnd when she kept her eyes lowered to her lap, he
raised her hand to his lips.

Charlotte looked up at him, her lips parting in
ιnconscious invitation.

"I always knew that," she whispered, and waited
ιn terror and excitement for the inevitable.

Devin kept hold of her hand as he lowered his head
:o hers and took her lips in a slow kiss. Charlotte
ɔecame suddenly aware that she was gripping his
ιand very tightly. She released it and his lips with a
ιittle "Oh!" of surprise. They looked into each other's
ǝyes for a few moments; then it was Charlotte who
ɔut her arms up around his neck and invited his

second kiss, deeper and more fervent than the first.
She pillowed her head contentedly on his shoulder
when he lifted his head again, and waited
expectantly for his declaration. He kissed her
temple, her ear, her neck where it joined her
shoulder, her throat.

"Tell me you have been only flirting with Charles
Adair," he murmured finally, laying his cheek
against the soft curls on top of her head.

"Flirting?" Charlotte's body stiffened slightly. Any
man who had been more into the petticoat line than
Devin Northcott would have immediately recognized
the danger signs. Devin was in blissful ignorance.

"You are young and devilish pretty," he continued,
running his free hand up and down the soft skin of
her arm, "and this is your come-out Season. Ain't
unnatural that you should try out your charms on
several young men. I am not angry with you. Hope
you can tell me, though, that your feelings for Adair
are no deeper than simple flirtation."

"I am much obliged to you, sir," Charlotte cried,
tearing herself out of his arms and rising from the
bench in order to sink into a deep curtsy in front of
him. "What charming compliments. I am young and
pretty. I beg your pardon, '*devilish*' pretty, I believe
you said. And I am a flirt? And you forgive me, sir?
You are not even angry with me? I do wish you had
chosen a less dusty spot for these charming declara-
tions, Mr. Northcott, for I feel I should sink to my
knees and kiss your feet in gratitude." Her voice was
quite shrill by this time.

Devin was by now also on his feet. "Charlotte, my
dear," he said aghast, reaching out a hand to her,
"believe me, I did not mean—"

"That I am young and *devilish* pretty? Oh, make no

apology, sir. I know it was the night and the moonlight that made you speak so foolishly."

"Charlotte, I—"

"Want a little more *flirtation*, sir? My apologies, but you have had your quota for tonight. I must rush back to the ball and find more young men to flirt with." She turned with a rustle of skirts and started toward the pathway.

Devin grasped her by the arm and jerked her around, none too gently, to face him. "Charlotte, will you stop behaving like a child and listen to me?" he began, not too wisely.

"Sir, do *children* flirt?" she asked icily, tossing her head.

"No, but they sometimes get a good thrashing," he parried, matching ice with ice.

"Threats, Mr. Northcott?" Charlotte asked disdainfully.

Devin expelled an exasperated breath. "Women! Deuced if I can understand them," he said.

"Might I suggest that you not even try, sir?" she suggested.

"Miss Wells," he said with a formal bow, having built up a fresh supply of ice, "allow me to escort you back to your friends." He extended his arm, which she ignored. Back straight, shoulders back, chin high, and heart crying in mortal agony, Charlotte stalked along the wooded path ahead of him until they reached open ground. Before Devin could take his leave of her, she was in the midst of a gay crowd of young people, her hand being eagerly solicited for the next country dance.

Lord Brampton had also succeeded in getting the partner of his choice for the second waltz of the

evening. For hours, it seemed, he had spent his
energies on ensuring that his tenants and his guests
were enjoying themselves. He felt no guilt now in
devoting himself to his own pleasures. He took his
wife in his arms and let the music create its own
rhythm in their bodies. She was a divine dancer; he
had noticed that on previous occasions. She was so
light on her feet, so tiny and slender, so receptive to
the guidance of her partner, that a man could relax
and lose his fear of treading on her toes or the hem of
her gown, or of losing her altogether on an intricate
turn.

Brampton held his wife quite close. In the semi-
darkness of his own garden and in the midst of
people who were bent on having a good time rather
than eyeing one another for food for gossip, he did
not care if he was being slightly improper. He held
her so that their bodily vibrations touched, even if
their bodies did not. He noticed with interest and
some hope that she made no effort to put a greater
distance between them. After a few minutes, in fact,
they were both lost to their surroundings, aware
only of each other and of the new and fragile rapport
between them.

Brampton was brought back to earth when he
found himself staring into the toothy grin of one of
his younger tenants. The lad yelled over the sounds
of the music and the conversation, "We'm hopin' you
does this every year, your lordship."

Brampton grinned. "I am glad to know you have
enjoyed the day, Tad," he said.

He looked down into his wife's quiet face. "Do you
have any pressing duties to perform after this dance,
my dear? Shall we walk up into the rose garden? I
believe we might find some solitude there."

Margaret was surprised, though she did not show

her feelings. "It would be good to get away from the press of people for a while, Richard," she said. She took his arm and leaned on him as they strolled from the dance floor up the sloping lawn toward the house, past the refreshment tables, where they smiled and nodded to friends, and finally angled off into the rose garden.

It was one area that had not been lit for the evening. Brampton knew that it was a favorite spot of his wife's. He had not wanted it to become public property on that evening. But it was still an area of great beauty. The heady perfume of roses hung on the night air. Bushes and blooms were caught by the moonlight and the fountain of water spouting from the mouth of a fat and naked cherub and falling into a stone basin sparkled.

They walked arm in arm along the quiet gravel walk until they came to the fountain. They stood looking at it; Brampton trailed a hand in the water of the basin.

"Well, my dear," he said, "do you feel that the day has been a success?"

"Yes, I do, Richard," she replied. "I believe everyone has had an enjoyable time."

"And that is very important to you, is it not?" he said, smiling down at her.

"Of course it is. It seems to me to be a responsibility to be one of the rich and privileged. In some ways it is not fair, is it? We should share when we have the chance."

"And do you feel privileged, my dear?"

"Indeed I do," she said earnestly. "Look at all I have." She indicated, with a sweep of her arm, the garden, the grounds beyond, and the house.

"And what about your own happiness?" he asked. "Do you ever think of yourself?"

"Of course," she replied, looking up at him wide-eyed.

He framed her face with his hands and kept it turned up toward him. He gazed down into those large gray eyes that always made him somehow catch his breath. "I wonder," he mused. "Am I the husband you would have chosen for yourself, my dear?"

She stared back into his eyes and swallowed painfully. "I did choose you, Richard," she said. "I refused three offers before you. I was not afraid of being an old maid."

"My dear, sweet little Meg," he said, his voice low and unsteady, "I do not deserve you, you know." He continued to hold her head in gentle hands as he brought his mouth down to cover hers.

Margaret was frightened. Now he would know; he would recognize her. But thoughts and feelings were soon dulled as she realized how different this kiss was from any others she had shared with him. It was a kiss of infinite gentleness and warmth and tenderness. She allowed her hands to spread from his chest to his shoulders so that she could rest her body against his. She felt safe, protected. Loved!

Brampton lifted his head and she noticed that his eyes were heavy-lidded and dreamy rather than blazing with passion as on other occasions. He moved his hands away from her face and wrapped his arms protectively around her. She rested her head against his shoulder, her face buried in the snowy folds of his neckcloth. They both closed their eyes and gave themselves up to the sensation of warmth and comfort.

Brampton should have noticed the similarity between the slender little body that he now held against him and the one he had made love to just a ew weeks previously. But, truth to tell, he had ardly spared a thought to his angel in the last week. ll he knew at the moment was that he held his wife, nat she was his, and that he loved her.

He kissed the side of her face. She did not move. Meg," he said softly against her ear, "will you look p at me?"

She moved her head from its comfortable resting lace and looked up, her hands still holding his houlders. But suddenly everything was not so eaceful. The stars were wheeling with dizzying notion above his head, dizzying enough to bring on a rave of nausea. Margaret grabbed at the tightly tretched fabric of Brampton's coat and felt herself uckle at the knees.

With an exclamation of alarm, Brampton held his rife against him with one arm while he slid the other eneath her knees and lifted her from the ground. Iis mind registered in dismay her tininess and ghtness. She could so easily slip away from him ltogether just at a time when he had realized that he was everything that was valuable in his world. Ie strode off with her in the direction of the house, gnoring the concerned exclamations of those guests ho saw him pass, and barking out commands to a tartled footman as soon as he reached the hall-ay.

"Fetch Doctor Pearson to my wife's room immedi-tely, Smithers," he said. "He is somewhere in the arden. And send up Kitty."

Margaret returned to consciousness as Brampton as carrying her up the stairs. She did not move. It lt so comfortable to be held in his strong arms, her ead pillowed comfortably on his broad shoulder. he reached out for him when he put her down ently on her bed, feeling bereft.

"Lie still, my love," he told her. "Kitty will be her
in a moment to put you comfortable and I have sen
for Doctor Pearson." His fingers were ineffectivel
tackling her hairdo in an attempt to unwrap th
braids from the back of her head so that she coul
rest more comfortably against the pillows.

"There was really no need, Richard," she said. "
am just very tired. But I am sorry to have spoiled th
evening."

"You have spoiled nothing, my dear," he said. "]
is well past midnight, and our guests do not need u
to ensure their enjoyment."

Kitty came rushing into the room at that momen
breathless and embarrassed to find Lord Brampto
sitting on the edge of her lady's bed, his hands in he
hair. She curtsied hastily.

"Ah, Kitty," he said, "your mistress is unwell. Sh
just fainted in the garden. Help her to undres
please. I shall bring the doctor here as soon a
Smithers has found him."

"Yes, my lord," Kitty said, and bustled to the be
where Margaret was lying very still and very pal
"What is it, my lady?" she scolded. "I told you yo
should have rested this afternoon. You have bee
overdoing things in the last week or two."

Margaret smiled wanly and allowed Kitty t
remove her clothing and help her into her nigh
gown. She also lifted her head while Kitty unpinne
the coils of braids and laid one plait over eac
shoulder.

Margaret lay outwardly placid when Brampton le
Doctor Pearson into the room. Somehow the docto
was carrying his black bag. She felt an inward wav
of amusement, realizing that the doctor must be i
the habit of taking it with him wherever he wen

even when he was invited out to dine and to dance. Brampton left the room again.

It seemed to Margaret a strangely inopportune time to find out for certain that she was with child—during the early hours of the morning, the windows bright with lantern light, the outdoors loud with voices and music, the doctor in evening clothes.

She stole a glance at Kitty, standing stolidly in the background. Her lips were pursed knowingly. It was impossible to fool one's lady's maid, she reflected. Kitty had probably known before she did!

"Well, your ladyship," Doctor Pearson said heartly as he repacked his bag, "I wager your husband will be the proudest man in the county by tomorrow morning."

Margaret blushed. "Doctor Pearson," she said, "please, will you say nothing to my husband? I wish to tell him myself."

He laughed jovially. "I know all about young love, your ladyship," he said. "I shall not spoil your secret."

"Thank you," she said, and closed her eyes.

Kitty led the doctor from the room. Margaret lay in quietness for a few minutes, until she heard the door open again. She opened her eyes as Brampton approached the bed.

"How do you feel, my dear?" he asked.

"Better, thank you, Richard," she said.

"Doctor Pearson seems to think all you need is rest," he said. "I am sorry, my dear. I should have insisted sooner that you not work so hard. For tomorrow, I must insist that you remain in bed."

"But our guests are still here, Richard."

"They are not children. They can amuse themselves. And I have a feeling that everyone will be too

tired tomorrow to need much amusing. No, my dear
you will stay here. Consider it a command, if you
will." He smiled faintly.

"Yes, Richard."

"You must sleep now, my dear. And do not worry
about the ball. I shall return outside and play the
host." He turned to leave the room.

"Richard?" she said on impulse.

He turned. "Yes, my dear?"

"Richard . . . It has been a lovely day, has it not?"

"Yes," he agreed softly. He hesitated, then leaned
over her and kissed her forehead. "Good night," he
said.

"Good night, Richard."

The draft Doctor Pearson had given her was taking
effect almost before Brampton left the room.
Margaret felt herself sink into a welcome fuzziness.
Of all the teeming details of the day's happenings,
her mind latched on to a very minor one for its last
conscious thought.

He called me Meg, she thought, and plunged into a
deep sleep.

13

TWO DAYS LATER all the house guests had left Brampton Court except the dowager countess and Charles. Margaret had got up to see them on their way. It seemed that all had enjoyed themselves; some seemed almost reluctant to leave. Annabelle whispered to Margaret when the latter was kissing her cheek in farewell that Ted Kemp was to call on her papa when they arrived back in the city for permission to pay his addresses to her. Susanna took a lingering farewell of Charles and hoped that he would come to call when he returned to town.

It was midafternoon by the time all the carriages had been seen on their way. Brampton turned to his wife and offered her his arm.

"Would you care to walk in the air for a few minutes, my dear?" he asked.

They strolled in the direction of the rose garden, leaving Charles to accompany the dowager and Charlotte into the house for tea.

"You are looking much better," Brampton commented. "You even have roses in your cheeks."

"I am afraid all the excitement and preparations proved too much for me," Margaret said placidly. "I feel fine now. I felt most lazy for those two days I spent in bed."

"The gardener tells me there are some new buds here," he said. "Let us find them."

They chattered amicably for an hour or more. Brampton explained to his wife that now that his guests had left, he was planning to get busy with plans to drain the marsh on the northwest corner of the estate. He was, in fact, hoping to leave for London within the next day or two to consult with an engineer and to engage his services. They returned to the house and went to their separate rooms to dress for dinner without one word of a personal nature having passed between them.

Margaret sat before her dressing-table mirror while Kitty patiently brushed out her waist-length hair and rebraided it. She stared sightlessly at her own reflection, trying not to give in to a mood of depression.

What was the matter with her that she could not hold her husband's attention? She felt over the last few weeks in the country that they were growing closer. On the day of the fair she had been convinced of it. Surely she could not have imagined the look of tenderness in his eyes on that night. He had kissed her for the first time (knowing it was she), and it had felt like a loving kiss. He had called her by name for the first time, and he had even used the shortened form that only her family had used before. And Margaret remembered the real alarm that had been in his voice as he had called out his orders to the footman when he was carrying her upstairs to her room. It had been such a magical night. If only she had not chosen such an inopportune time to faint!

But she had fully expected Richard to come to her the next day and call her Meg and look at her with the new tenderness. She had pictured him sitting on the edge of her bed and holding her hand as she told him about their child. Then he would hold her and kiss her again and tell her that he loved her. And they would live happily ever after.

Instead, she had waited until well into the afternoon and then he had come and stood beside her bed for no longer than five minutes and had called her "my dear." He had asked after her health, had forbidden her to get up either for dinner or during the next day, and had left. She had not seen him for the rest of the day. And yesterday had seen a repeat performance.

Margaret had been bitterly disappointed—and she still held the secret of her pregnancy. She had hoped desperately that today, when Richard had finally allowed her downstairs to bid good-bye to their guests, he would treat her again with the intimacy that had begun three days before. Her hopes had soared when he had suggested a walk and then had led her directly to the rose garden. She had thought his suggestion a deliberate attempt to recapture the atmosphere of that earlier occasion when she had spoiled an intimate moment.

Yet all he had done was look at her new rosebuds with her and talk about his drainage schemes. And she was still just "my dear." They had strolled past the fountain as if it were just any fountain anywhere.

Margaret could have cried with vexation. Had he changed his mind? Had his behavior of the other night been motivated only by the music and the moonlight and the smell of roses? Had it only been wishful thinking to imagine that he was growing to love her?

In his own room, Brampton was feeling equally dissatisfied with the way things had gone in the last few days. He had been worried about his wife, but had concluded that the doctor must be right in saying that it was really only rest that she needed. After his insisting that she stay in bed for two days, she was looking better today. Some color had returned to her cheeks.

But in those two days they had returned to their former relationship, all trace of the warmth that had been growing between them gone. He had realized fully on the night of the fair that he loved his wife—loved her as a whole person. He loved her character, her sweetness, her quietness, her kindness; he loved her appearance, the slender daintiness of her, the heart-shaped face with the large, calm eyes, and the heavy brown braids; and he wanted her with more sexual longing than he had ever wanted any woman —even his angel, incredible as it seemed to him.

On that night he had believed that she felt the same way. He remembered the way she had danced with him, as if she shared in perfect harmony the rhythm of his body, and the way she had clung to his arm as they walked to the rose garden, and the way her body had fitted itself to his of her own free will when he kissed her. He remembered that she had not pulled away from him when the kiss was over, but had nestled her head on his shoulder and had seemed contented to be held.

Brampton had felt desire rise in him as they had stood there. He had been about to tell her that he loved her, about to suggest that they abandon their guests to their own devices for a while and return to the house. He had wanted to take her to his own bed and make love to her.

It had seemed to him that it was a singularly inopportune time for her to faint! And why had she done so? Could tiredness after all the busy activity of the previous few weeks entirely explain it? Was it possible that she had been frightened by the passion

she could feel developing in their relationship? Was
she contented to let things remain as they always had
been? And yet her manner in the bedroom after the
doctor had seen her had seemed unusually tender.

When he had visited her the next day, Brampton
had been nervous and unsure of himself. He did not
know how he should behave. He had decided to take
his cue from her. He had hoped desperately that she
would smile at him, perhaps even hold out her arms
to him, or at least show by her expression that she
remembered the night before and wished to continue
what they had started.

But there had been nothing. She had been lying on
her back, the bedcovers drawn up under her arms,
her hands clasped loosely over one another, her face
with its usual expression of calm. Her eyes had
watched him as he approached the bed, but there
was nothing in them to encourage him. He had stood
there formally, asking about her health, playing the
heavy-handed lord and master by ordering her to
remain in bed, leaving after five minutes, when he
had really wanted to sit down beside her, draw her
into his arms, and . . .

Brampton gave a loud exclamation of disgust and
threw from him the third ruined neckcloth. Stevens
patiently handed him another freshly laundered and
freshly starched one and watched resignedly as his
master proceeded to mangle that one too. He knew
there was no point in offering to make the knot and
arrange the folds himself. His lordship always
insisted on dressing himself.

Brampton gave himself a mental shakedown.
Earlier that afternoon he had been determined to
force the issue. She was up again and looking well;
their guests had left; they had an hour in which to be
alone before they need think of dressing for dinner.

He decided to take her back to the rose garden, to see if he could rekindle that sympathy there had been between them there three evenings before. At least he must say something to her, find out if there was any chance that she could grow to love him.

Instead he had been like a nervous schoolboy, afraid to broach the subject uppermost in his mind, not knowing how to begin, terrified of being rejected or—worse—of having her placid eyes turn on him in incomprehension. He had prattled on about his plans for draining the marsh; how much less romantic could he get! The trouble was that she was such a damned good listener, so interested and sympathetic. Before he had known it, he had really warmed to his subject, and the time seemed totally wrong for trying to broach more personal matters.

So it still remained for this unseen barrier between his wife and himself to be broken down. Would the time ever be right? And he was planning to leave tomorrow for a few days in London.

Later that evening, the three ladies were alone in the blue salon. Lord Brampton and his brother were still in the dining room drinking their port. The dowager settled herself close to the fire she had requested, though it seemed to the other two ladies unnecessary on so warm a night. She was working at some needlepoint. Charlotte had wandered over to the pianoforte and was picking out a tune with one finger. Margaret followed her across the room and stood behind the piano bench.

"Do you wish me to bring some music, Lottie?" she asked.

Charlotte sighed and stopped playing. "No," she said, "I do not wish to play."

"Are you missing the company?"

"No, not really, Meg. I think it is time I returned to Mama and Papa."

"Lottie! I thought you would be contented to live with Richard and me until—well, until you are settled for yourself."

"I—I do not wish to sound ungrateful," Charlotte said, pressing down the piano keys at random with the fingers of her right hand, "but I am homesick, Meg."

Margaret looked at her sister in astonishment and felt a sharp stab of guilt. Lottie's voice was so lifeless, so unhappy, so unlike her usual self! How long had she been this way? Had it happened only today as a result of the guests leaving? Or had something happened to cause the change? Margaret could not be at all certain of the anwers to her own questions. She realized that almost ever since they had retired to the country she had been so busy with the entertainment of their guests and the organization of the Fair, and she had been so wrapped up in her own unsatisfactory relationship with Richard, that she had almost totally neglected her sister. And the whole idea of the house party had been to entertain Lottie. Margaret had just naturally assumed that her normally exuberant sister was enjoying herself. She seemed to be a girl that just did not have problems.

Margaret sat down beside her sister on the bench and spoke quietly so that her mother-in-law would not overhear. "What is wrong, Lottie?" she asked.

"Oh, nothing," Charlotte said, attempting to smile. "I am just blue-deviled. I need a change of scene, Meg."

"Is it Charles?"

"Charles?"

"Has he not come up to scratch, Lottie? He seems to favor your company so much that I must admit I had expected some declaration before now."

"Charles?" Charlotte repeated, looking up startled. "Oh, Meg, you are quite out there. Charles just likes my company because—well, just because. He is just a friend, Meg. We do not like each other in *that* way."

Margaret felt even more guilty. Here was the little sister that she had always thought she knew inside out. "Are you bamming me?" she asked. "But, Lottie, there *is* someone, is there not?"

Charlotte resumed her absentminded effort to pick out a tune on the keyboard.

"Is it Mr. Northcott, Lottie?"

"Perhaps you could bring me some music, Meg."

"Lottie, is it?"

"I don't wish ever to talk about him. He is conceited and he is not a gentleman."

"Mr. Northcott?"

Charlotte did not reply.

"What has he done, Lottie?" Margaret persisted. "Has he been bothering you? Has he been trying to make love to you?"

Charlotte put her hands in her lap and looked down at them. "He called me a flirt."

"What? But why?"

"Because he is a horrid man and unmannerly and I hate him," Charlotte said, leaping restlessly to her feet and crossing the room to the fireplace. "These are such lovely colors you are stitching into your picture, Lady Brampton," she said with false heartiness to the dowager.

Margaret was left sitting on the piano bench. She was surprised and puzzled by the strange turn of events. She had thought that the early attraction between her sister and Devin Northcott had died a natural death a long while before. And she had been sure that there was a strong bond been Charlotte and Charles, though she had been a little puzzled by his slowness in coming to the point. She could not at the moment imagine what the very correct and very gentlemanly Mr. Northcott could possibly have done to deserve the outburst that Lottie had just indulged in. But one thing was startlingly clear: her sister was very much in love with her husband's friend!

The Earl of Brampton left for London late the following morning. He planned to be away for three or four days. He spent the whole of his journey wishing that he had asked his wife to go with him, while realizing that he could not have done so without having caused a great upheaval. Charlotte would have had to come, too. Margaret was also wishing he had asked her to accompany him, though she too realized that she could not have gone.

Charlotte had agreed the night before to stay at Brampton Court until the earl returned. She did sit down in the morning, though, and write to her parents to tell them to expect her at home about one week later. She was mortally depressed. She had been so close to capturing her man on the night of the fair. She had experienced her first kiss on that night and she had loved it—and him! And then had come that stupid quarrel. She still blamed Devin. How dare he accuse her of being a flirt! How could he be so conceited and so stuffy—and so wrong!

Yet Charlotte knew that in reacting as she had, she had lost all chance of winning Devin. Was her pride worth so high a cost? He had been to the house only once since that night. He had come to dinner on the night before all the guests left. He had talked amiably to everyone, even that odious *flirt*, Susanne Kemp. But he had ignored her, if one discounted an infinitesimal and stiff bow in her direction when she had first entered the drawing room before dinner. She had made no effort to talk to him, either, but she had had a perfectly good reason. After all, he had insulted her.

The annoying thing was that she still loved him. Her first instinct had been to leave Hampshire as soon as she possibly could, to run home as far from Devin Northcott as she could get. But she had to confess to herself as she agreed to stay with Meg until his lordship came home, that she hoped something might happen in that time to patch up the quarrel.

Charles was restless. It was several weeks since he had last heard from his Juana. In that last letter, she had been confident that soon she would be on her way to England. She had written that she would inform him as soon as she arrived in Portsmouth. He had not had time to inform her that he was removing to the country, but he had left careful instructions at his mother's home in London. As soon as a letter arrived there, a messenger was to post to Brampton Court with it. He was afraid that if he did not hear from Juana soon, he would have to make arrangements to rejoin his regiment in Spain. Then they would be in a tangle, with her traveling to England while he returned to Spain.

He was explaining this frustrating situation to Charlotte the morning after the earl had left for London. They were sitting at the edge of the lake half a mile distant from the house. Their horses were tethered to a tree nearby, grazing peacefully on the grass that was within their reach.

Margaret had felt a little guilty allowing the two young people to ride off together unchaperoned. But she was busy; she was sorting through all the household linen with Mrs. Foster. She was determined to use the days while Richard was away to do many of the tasks she had been intending to do ever since she had arrived. She wanted the time to pass quickly. She reassured herself, though, with the knowledge that there was no romance between Lottie and Charles.

Charles had a handful of stones and was skipping them across the water. "So you can see why I am getting worried," he said to his companion. "I don't know what I shall do."

"I am sure you will hear from her soon," Charlotte reassured him. "At least you know that she loves you, Charles. You are sure, are you not?"

"Oh, not a doubt of it," he laughed. "She says I am the only one who will stand up to her. When she yells, I yell right back."

"Goodness!" Charlotte commented. "Do you think it wise to marry?"

"There will never be a dull moment," he said cheerfully. "I shall probably beat her daily, but you can be sure she will give as good as she gets."

"Goodness!"

"And what about you, Charlotte, my love? I had great hopes for you when I saw you and Northcott slinking off into the greenery the other night. I was in eager expectation of an announcement before the evening was out. And then I saw you holding court to a veritable army of young sparks, Northcott nowhere in sight. And we have hardly seen him since. Can it be that Juana and I are not the only ones to have blazing rows?"

"He is just stuffy and insufferably high in the instep," Charlotte said.

Charles raised his eyebrows and his throwing arm paused. "Strong words, my love. I take it you still love him, then?"

"I hate him!"

"Yes, quite. Can it be, Charlotte, that the oh-so-proper Mr. Northcott made *improper* advances? Did you send him way with a swollen cheek?"

"He accused me of flirting, Charles," she said indignantly, "with you."

"Indeed? I tell you what, Charlotte. He must be in love too. Jealousy and all that."

Charlotte said nothing for a while. She absently counted the number of times each stone skipped across the water.

"Do you really think so, Charles?" she asked wistfully at last.

"Eh? Think what? Oh, Northcott? Yes, no doubt about it. You're quite a fetching little thing, you know. I might have fallen for you myself if I hadn't already left my heart with a certain Spanish termagant."

"Am I supposed to be flattered?" she asked doubtfully. "But listen, Charles, I really do need a plan."

"Oh, oh, that sounds dangerous," he said. He picked up a fresh handful of stones and continued to throw them across the water.

A few minutes later, Charlotte gave a loud exclamation of triumph.

"Now look what you made me do," her companion complained. "Spoiled my aim completely and ruined my average. That one did not bounce at all."

"I have it!" she announced excitedly. "When you hear from Juana, I shall come with you to Portsmouth to meet her, though of course I shan't tell anyone I'm going and I shall leave a note for Meg so that she will not worry, but she will not give away your secret, and we shall all come back the next day and you will be excited introducing her to your mother and my brother-in-law, and I shall be delighted too, you see, and everyone will know that I must have known about her all along if I went with you to meet her, and then Mr. Northcott will know that I never was flirting with you if I went with you to meet your betrothed and then he will have to beg my pardon and tell me that he loves me, and he will ask for my hand and everything will be all right. See?"

Charles was gaping at her. "No, I do not see," he said. "Would you mind repeating that? No," he said, holding up a hand as she took a deep breath and opened her mouth again, "don't repeat it. Explain it a different way. And take a breath somewhere along the way, will you, Charlotte, love?"

She wriggled impatiently. "Don't you see?" she said. "It's perfect. When you go to Portsmouth, I shall go with you."

"Hold it right there," he ordered. "That's a scatter-brained idea, if I ever heard one."

"Why?"

"Why, she asks," he said, eyes raised to the sky. "You do not ride around England with a man and no chaperone, my dear."

"Phooey. It would take only a few hours to get there and then I will be with Juana and her servants."

"And what if, by some accident, we were forced to spend a night on the road? You would be hopelessly compromised, my love. I should be forced to marry you and it would be good-bye, Juana, and good-bye, Devin. Perhaps we could introduce them to each other."

"Nonsense," Charlotte said. "For what possible reason could we be delayed on the road?"

"Earthquake. Typhoon. Snowstorm."

"In July? How foolish!"

"Very well. Continue," he said with mock weariness.

"I should leave a note for Meg so that she would not worry," she continued. "But Meg will not give away your secret. But you see, Charles, when I return with you and Juana, everyone will see that I am pleased and that I must have known about her all along."

" 'Everyone' being Devin Northcott, I assume?"

"Well, yes. Anyway, he will be forced to admit then that I could not have been flirting with you, will he not? And then he will be very sorry."

"And grovel in the dirt at your feet and beg for the honor of your hand. What an addlepated female you are, Charlotte."

"Why?" she asked crossly.

"He is much more likely to turn up his aristocratic nose in disgust at a female who would go traipsing around with another man."

"He would not. And don't make him sound so odious."

"Sorry, but I thought he was 'stuffy and insufferably high in the instep.' Anyway, my love, the answer is no. You will have to think of something else."

"No?"

"No!"

"But, Charles—"

"Absolutely and irrevocably NO my love. A strong, strong negative. The opposite of yes."

"Oh!"

14

CHARLOTTE WAS SITTING beside Charles in a closed
carriage belonging to the Earl of Brampton. She was
huddled inside a thin summer pelisse that covered
her favorite yellow muslin dress, the one that made
her look like a ray of sunshine, according to one
admirer. She felt cold and cross. The rain and the
mist seemed to have penetrated even the carriage so
that she was chilled, and her hair under its yellow
bonnet felt as if it had lost some of its curl and
bounce. She was certainly not going to be at her best
to meet Juana. To crown it all, Charles was stiff and
starchy and cross as a bear.

It was two days after their conversation at the
lake. Finally that morning Charles had received the
letter he had long awaited. He and Charlotte had
been in the stables preparing to take their horses for
a ride, when a figure familiar to Charles from his
mother's establishment in London came riding in on
a well-lathered horse.

"John!" Charles had greeted him eagerly, striding
toward the new arrival and grabbing the horse by the
reins. "You have news?"

"A letter for you from Portsmouth, Captain," John
had replied, slipping from the saddle with a thankful
sigh and withdrawing a package from an inner
pocket.

Charles had whipped it from his grasp and had eagerly torn open its seals. Charlotte had come running to his side. "She's here, Charlotte," he had cried. "At Portsmouth. The Crown and Anchor."

Charlotte had clapped her hands. "How exciting! Are we setting out immediately?"

Charles had ignored her choice of pronoun. "She has a duenna with her and a manservant and some sort of male second cousin. And doubtless two mountains of luggage. I shall need two carriages."

"Take one from here and hire an additional post chaise for the return journey," Charlotte had suggested.

"Good idea," he had mused. "If I start immediately I should be in Portsmouth by midafternoon. We should be back here by midevening."

"Will you just give me time to change out of my riding habit?" Charlotte had asked anxiously.

"Eh? You have all day to change, my love. We won't be back here for hours."

"No, Charles, please," she had pleaded, catching at his arm. "You must let me go. It is my only chance, don't you see?"

"No, I don't see, Charlotte," he had answered unsympathetically. "And I have no time to stand here arguing. I have several arrangements to make."

"I shall keep asking until you change your mind," Charlotte had said, clinging to his arm tenaciously. "Charles, be fair! You are having your chance with Juana. Let me have mine with Devin."

"I don't know what makes you think this featherbrained scheme will bring him running to your side," Charles had said in exasperation, "but come if you must. On your own head be it, Charlotte. Just don't expect me to marry you when your reputation is gone, that's all."

"Oh, thank you, Charles," she had said excitedly, aiming a kiss at his cheek and missing entirely.

"You can have half an hour, not one minute longer," Charles had yelled at her as she began to hurry toward the house. "And don't forget to leave a note for Margaret, or Dick will have my head."

Charlotte had been ready with three minutes to spare. She had dressed carefully and touched up her hair, all without summoning Kitty. She had not wanted anyone to spoil her plan now that it looked like succeeding. She had spent five minutes composing a very careful letter to Meg, explaining everything and begging her to keep the secret until the evening. Margaret had not been at home. She had gone, with the dowager, to visit some sick cottage tenants. At the last moment she had grabbed a pelisse. Heavy clouds had moved across the sun; it looked as if it might rain later on.

Charles was regretting his decision to allow Charlotte to accompany him. Nothing but trouble could come of it. It was just not the thing for him to allow an unattached, unaccompanied female to ride in a closed carriage with him, especially for such a long time and distance. He knew that there would be big trouble with Dick. Even his gentle sister-in-law would surely express her displeasure. They would, of course, blame him. He was old enough to know better, even if Charlotte was not. As if he was not going to have a difficult-enough time as it was, suddenly producing a Spanish girl and her entourage and introducing her as his fiancée. What a hobble! His mother would throw a fit of the vapors per minute!

His mood was not lightened by the rain. It made the inside of the carriage clammy, and he could imagine what it was doing to the outside. He had so hoped that his darling would see England at its best when he took her to his childhood home. This reminded him uncomfortably of Spain in the rainy season and all those long and pointless forced marches to and fro across the country playing cat and mouse with Boney and the French.

Fortunately, at least, these English roads were still passable in the rain. They changed horses once at a posting inn, arranging to pick up the Earl of Brampton's cattle on the return journey. They arrived in Portsmouth at three o'clock in the afternoon and were directed to the Crown and Anchor Inn.

For a long time Charlotte had been forming in her mind a mental image of Charles' betrothed. She had a firm picture of a girl about the same height and build as Meg, but with very dark hair and eyes. She was surprised, therefore, when she was ushered into a private parlor ahead of Charles and saw a girl rise from a chair close to the fire. She was dark, yes, with masses of black hair coiled on top of her head, and flashing eyes that looked equally black. But she was tall—surely on a level with Charles' chin—and had a luscious figure: heavy breasts, tiny waist, full hips. She looked almost frighteningly haughty, her body held very straight, her chin high, her heavy black eyebrows raised in apparent disdain.

All these things Charlotte noted in a flash. A moment later, this haughty aristocrat was hurtling across the room, shrieking "Carlos!" and a whole string of other Spanish words that were incomprehensible to Charlotte. Charlotte had the presence of mind to step aside before the human missile hurled herself against Charles and was picked up by the waist and twirled around and around. He clasped her to him as if he would break every bone in her body, and murmured Spanish words into her ear.

Charlotte could not understand and, anyway, was a little embarrassed by this public display of affection. She turned and examined with interest the two other occupants of the room. One was an older lady dressed all in black, her graying black hair drawn severely back from her face and tied in a topknot. She looked as aristocratic as Juana, though Charlotte assumed she was the deunna. The other was a man in his forties, Charlotte guessed, also tall and thin, with a sallow face, graying hair, and high prominent cheekbones. He must be the second cousin, Charlotte guessed. Both were looking disapprovingly at the demonstration going on before their eyes.

In the meantime, a burst of Spanish had broken loose from the couple who were still clasped together, though it looked as if Juana was trying to pull free. It became obvious almost immediately that she was furiously angry. It was equally obvious that Charles was amused. As she prattled on, he grabbed her arms and shook her gently, laughing and talking calmly back at her in her own language.

"She is jealous of you, Charlotte, my love," he said at last. "She thinks you must be the reason I have been so long coming to fetch her." And he laughed gaily and entered the fray again. The duenna had moved closer to the couple and was also talking, apparently in an effort to calm her mistress. The cousin continued to stare disapprovingly from his position of safety across the room.

Juana raised her hand and brought it viciously toward Charles' cheek. He caught her wrist and prevented the blow, but his face sobered instantly. He waved his other hand in front of her face and talked in fast, crisp Spanish. Charlotte looked on in astonishment. He was obviously threatening to strike Juana. Could this be the boyish, devil-may-care Charles that she knew? She had hardly seen him serious.

Juana's hysterics ended almost immediately. She flung her arms around Charles' neck and proceeded to sob loudly on his shoulder. He winked outrageously at the duenna over her head, and the older lady nodded in sober approval.

"Come and be introduced, Charlotte, my love," he offered finally when the sobs had been replaced by the occasional sniffle. "This is Juana. Is she not magnificent?"

Juana, in a burst of generous contrition, tore herself from Charles' arms and flung her arms around Charlotte. She favored her with a long, excited speech.

"I have to confess that she is thanking you for not loving me," Charles translated with smug amusement. "She cannot imagine how you could have shown such fortitude."

Charlotte smiled, nodded, and seriously thought that Charles must have windmills in his head to be contemplating matrimony with this not-so-dormant volcano.

The reunion quickly gave place to business. Charles spoke to all three of the Spaniards, apparently instructing them to pack their belongings and be ready to leave as soon as possible. After a few minutes they left the parlor, Juana with great reluctance. She beckoned Charlotte to go with her, but Charles said something and restrained his traveling companion with a hand on the arm.

"I told her we are tired and thirsty," he explained. "I shall order tea for you and something for myself and then you may join Juana and her maid upstairs while I see about hiring an extra carriage. Isn't she just marvelous, Charlotte?"

"She is certainly unique," Charlotte commented diplomatically.

Charles chuckled and rang the bell for service. He gave their order to the girl who appeared, and asked her to hurry. Charlotte sank into the chair that the duenna had vacated, close to the fire. Charles crossed the room, seated himself on the arm of her chair, and placed a hand on her shoulder.

"Charlotte, my love," he said, leaning toward her and looking into her face.

And it was these words and this sight that met the anxious ears and eyes of the Countess of Brampton and Devin Northcott as they burst into the room.

Margaret had returned from her morning of visiting, watched the dowager climb the stairs to her room to change for luncheon, gone into the rose garden to cut some fresh buds for the dining-room table, and finally retired to her room to wash her hands, tidy her hair, and change her gown. She noticed immediately the white envelope propped against the mirror of her dressing table. She slit open the envelope and read the letter over which Charlotte had labored for five whole minutes and which she had been convinced explained the situation clearly.

Dearest Meg,

Pray forgive me for any worry I may cause you, but I have gone with Charles to Portsmouth. He is in love, Meg, as you will soon be forced to admit for yourself. Even his lordship cannot be angry when he knows that. I know you may be cross with me, Meg; I should not really do this. But my case is hopeless. This is the only chance I have of any sort of happiness. You know yourself that I do not love Charles, but everyone else thinks that I do, you see, dearest. All will be explained when we arrive home again. Your own dear sister,

                                        Charlotte

Margaret read the letter through a second time, panic rising in her, hoping there was some other interpretation to put on it than the obvious one. She put a shaking hand to her mouth, trying to think clearly enough to know what to do. If only Richard were at home! She finally rushed along to the dowager's room and knocked hastily on the door.

"Mama, I have found this letter in my room," she gasped out. "Charlotte has eloped with Charles. They are on their way to the Continent to be married—at least, I assume they plan to marry."

The dowager crossed the room with uncharacteristic haste, forgetting hartshorn and vinaigrette in this real crisis, and snatched the letter from Margaret's hand.

"What a pair of clothheads!" was her first comment. "They will never suit, Margaret. They are just a pair of irresponsible children. And she does not even pretend to love him! What can it mean!"

"I fear she is marrying him in the hope of recovering from a disappointment," Margaret said.

"Devin, I suppose," the dowager agreed. "And it is he she should marry, too. He would probably take her over his knee and spank her every so often and beat some sense into her."

"But what are we to *do*, Mama?" Margaret wailed. "This would be a terrible mistake for both of them."

She did not wait for her mother-in-law's answer.

She had heard a horse approach up the driveway. "Richard!" she cried in relief, and fled out of the room, down the main staircase, and through the front door. She found herself confronting Devin Northcott, who was in the act of dismounting from his horse and handing the reins to a groom.

"Good afternoon, ma'am," he said. "Hope I haven't disturbed your luncheon. Came from m' mother to invite you all to dinner tomorrow evening. Bram should be home by then?"

"Oh, Mr. Northcott," Margaret sobbed, and startled him by rushing straight into his arms.

"I say, ma'am, what is it?" he asked, alarmed, and proceeded to help her up the steps and into the house.

"I do beg your pardon, sir," she said, "but I don't know what to do."

"Calm yourself, Lady Bram," he said soothingly, and led her into a small salon, closing the door behind them. "Tell me what's the matter. I shall do m' best to help."

"It's Charlotte," she wailed.

"What? Miss Wells? Ill? Hurt?"

"She has eloped with Charles. But she does not love him, Mr. Northcott. She is only unhappy because she has quarreled with you." Margaret was distraught. She would not normally have talked so indiscreetly to a man who was not even a member of the family.

Devin had turned pale and stood rooted to the spot. "Gretna?" he asked in a strangled voice.

"No, Portsmouth. They must be intending to cross the Channel."

"When? How long ago did they leave?"

"I don't know exactly. Maybe two hours. Probably less."

"I must follow them," Devin said, and started for the door. "Don't distress yourself, ma'am. I shall bring her home safe."

"Oh, but I must come with you," Margaret cried, grabbing for his arm.

"Wouldn't hear of it, ma'am," Devin said firmly. "Not at all the thing. And Bram wouldn't like it."

"Mr. Northcott," she said, "Charlotte is my sister. I must come. She will listen to me, I am sure. Besides, she seems to be without a female companion. She will need me. If we can be seen to return together, we may avert scandal."

Devin hesitated. "Must have a closed carriage, then. Will be slower, though. But probably best— coming on to rain. I shall go see to it, ma'am." And he hurried away in the direction of the stables while Margaret rushed up the stairs to tell the dowager what was happening and to fetch a cloak and bonnet and half-boots. Ten minutes later, the coach was on its way—the fast-traveling carriage that had brought the family from London, and the earl's best horses. By the time Charles and Charlotte arrived at the Crown and Anchor, Devin and Margaret were only half an hour behind them. They were fortunate enough to recognize the familiar carriage in the courtyard of the inn.

Margaret hurried to the public room of the inn, praying that they were in time, that the couple had not yet embarked on a ship for the Continent. Devin was close behind her, a reassuring hand on the small of her back as they met the landlord and inquired about the occupants of the plain carriage standing outside.

"In the private parlor," he replied absently and continued on his way to a tableful of customers, a tray of ale balanced on one hand.

"Thank God," Devin remarked as Margaret pushed at the door of the parlor, too overwrought with emotion to consider the courtesy of knocking first. The situation looked bad enough. Charles was sitting on the arm of Charlotte's chair, leaning toward her, a hand on her shoulder, calling her "my love." Both jumped guiltily to their feet.

"Lottie! Thank God we are in time!" Margaret exclaimed, and rushed across the room to clasp her sister in her arms.

"Meg?" Charlotte said simultaneously. "What are you doing here?"

The two men meanwhile were eyeing each other suspiciously.

Devin stood stiffly close to the door. "I shall want an explanation for this, Adair," he said sternly. "A lady's reputation at stake, y'know. Very bad *ton.*"

"She would come, the little hothead," Charles explained warily. "But I fail to see what business this is of yours, Northcott."

"Shan't discuss the matter with ladies present," Devin replied. "Shall ask you to step outside. I shall be calling you out over this, y'know."

"Mr. Northcott," Charlotte cried, tearing herself from her sister's arms and crossing the room to stand in front of him, "indeed I am to blame. Charles did not want to bring me, truly, but I would not let him be until he agreed."

He looked down at her coldly. "I shall have plenty to say to you too, Miss Wells, when I've finished with your—friend," he said. "You need a man who will keep a firm hand on your reins, ma'am, and I intend to be that man."

"Indeed!" Charlotte drew in a deep breath and seemed incapable of expelling it for a moment.

"Lottie, indeed you have behaved badly," Margaret

added in firm support of Devin. "You must know that an elopement will place you beyond the approval of society. And there is no need for it, love. We may not approve the match, but I am sure that neither Richard nor I would actively try to stop the marriage if you truly want to carry it through."

Charlotte stared back and forth between Devin and Margaret, openmouthed. "What elopement? What marriage?" she asked, puzzled.

Charles suddenly exploded into mirth from across the room. "Charlotte, my love, I'll bet it was the letter," he managed to get out between bursts of laughter. "You featherbrained little twit, I should have insisted on reading it. Margaret is obviously under the impression that you and I are eloping to the Continent together."

"How could they?" Charlotte asked. "You didn't think that, did you, Meg? But I told you in the letter that Charles loved Juana and that everyone would see it when we got back tonight. And I told you that I came only because . . . Well, I told you why I came, Meg."

"Who is Juana?" Margaret asked weakly.

"Margaret," Charles said, trying to contain his amusement, "will you come sit by the fire? Northcott, take a seat. I think I had better explain this mess to you myself."

Within five minutes the misunderstanding had been cleared up, though Margaret took it upon herself to scold both her sister and her brother-in-law for irresponsible behavior. Devin said not a word from his chair close to the door, nor did he return the shy, anxious glances that Charlotte cast in his direction from time to time. She had the feeling that her plan had come crashing around her ears and that he had taken her in disgust. She drew hope, however, from the masterful words he had spoken earlier in the conversation.

"We must see to getting back to Brampton Court tonight," Charles said finally. "I was about to go hire an extra post chaise when you two arrived."

"There will be no need," Margaret said. "We came in a carriage, too. Surely there will be enough room for everyone."

"I shall go see about the horses," he replied. "Charlotte, my love"—he missed the glower cast in his direction by Devin—"go upstairs to Juana and let her know by some sort of sign language that she should hurry and that my sister-in-law is here waiting to meet her."

They left together. Devin crossed the room and placed a hand on Margaret's shoulder. "All's well, Lady Bram," he said. "You can stop worrying. No one need ever know—not even Bram if you choose not to tell him." He leaned forward to gaze concernedly into her face.

This was the sight and these were the words that greeted the Earl of Brampton as he pushed open the door to the parlor.

15

THE EARL OF Brampton had spent a busy few days in London. He had to see his man of business about various matters relating to his several estates, and he had more than one meeting with an eminent engineer, arranging for the man to visit Brampton Court and make plans for draining the marsh. The drainage scheme would free many more acres of land for cultivation and would help his tenants to a more prosperous way of life.

Yet Brampton was not happy during those few days. As long as he was busy, he felt tolerably contented. But the house in Grosvenor Square felt empty and cheerless with no other occupants than the skeleton staff that was kept there during the summer months. Sitting in his library on the third evening, after an early return from a sparsely populated club, Brampton mused on the change that had occurred in him in just a few months. He vividly remembered getting embarrassingly drunk in this very room because his happy solitude was about to be shattered by a dull and insipid bride.

Dull and insipid! Meg! Sweet, sensible, and intelligent Meg? He found now that life was dull only without her. He got up restlessly from his chair, refilled his glass, and sipped its contents. He smiled ruefully at himself. Was he about to get drunk because he was forced to be away from her for a few days?

Brampton set the glass down firmly beside the brandy decanter and left the library. He went to his room and let Stevens help him off with his clothes and on with his nightshirt and dressing gown. He dismissed his valet before going to bed. He wandered aimlessly to the chair beside the empty fireplace. How restless he felt! How he needed his wife, even the little she had so far been prepared to give of herself.

Brampton got to his feet again, opened the door into the dressing room that connected his bedchamber with his wife's, and then the door into her room. He wandered inside. The room was very tidy, very empty. He crossed to the bed and sat on its edge. He rubbed one hand lightly back and forth across the pillow. If only she were there. He made a decision as he sat there not to spent another night away from home—and home now meant wherever Meg was. Although he had a full day of business yet to transact, somehow he would speed through it so that he would have enough daylight hours left in which to ride back to Brampton Court.

His decision made, Brampton rose to leave his wife's room. He could sleep now. He smiled as he noticed a closet door slightly ajar, and crossed the room to close it. Something was in the way. He stooped to pick up a fan that had dropped to the floor and surveyed the rackful of ball gowns that had been left behind because they would not be needed in the country. He smiled fondly down at the fan—his favorite, the wine-colored one. He could picture her so clearly flirting it in his direction while her eyes sparkled at him through the slits of the silver mask. He raised his arm to place it on a shelf.

Then Brampton froze! My God, that was not his wife's fan. It belonged to— He felt his heart pumping and was convinced that he had stepped straight into a nightmare. How had it got there? Had she been in the house, in his wife's room?

Brampton gazed frantically around the closet. He could see that one box on a top shelf had tipped forward, probably dislodged when something had been pulled from beneath it. The lid had shifted off the box; the fan could easily have slipped out of it.

Brampton had a sickening feeling of *déjà vu*. He knew before he lifted down the box what he would find inside; he knew the truth. Only his wife had been in her own room. His wife was his angel! By the time he had set the box on the bed and lifted the lid, he would have been surprised not to find the silver gown and mask and the powdered wig inside.

He sank onto the bed beside the box, all feeling mercifully dead inside him for a while. And yet he was struck with the thought of what a fool he had been. Now that he knew, the truth seemed so obvious that he was convinced he must have been blind. The same height, the same light, slender figure, the same response in himself, though it had been more physical in the case of his angel.

Shame and embarrassment were the first feelings to return. What a fool he had made of himself, making excuses to spend evenings away from Meg, just so that he could meet her in a clandestine manner and make passionate love to her in the darkness of Devin Northcott's bed. And that heart-wrenching good-bye—when he was to see her at the breakfast table a few hours later. His avoidance of his wife's bed because he felt he had sullied his honor in another woman's arms. My God, what a prize idiot he had made of himself!

How she must have laughed at him!

Fury was the feeling that finally came—and held. He had just been spending weeks setting his wife up on a pedestal, almost worshiping her for her perfections, and all the time she was a low little schemer. She had quite deliberately set him up as a fool. He had spent all the months of their marriage feeling guilt over his physical use of her, imagining that their intercourse was causing her displeasure and perhaps pain. And yet in reality she was an experienced little slut who had opened to him with more sexual abandon than any of the most practiced lightskirts that he had ever taken to bed. Brampton viciously relived that last night of love, forgetting the first and his feeling then that she was in fact untutored in the arts of lovemaking.

Was she in the habit of such behavior? Brampton wondered. Was he the only man she had diguised herself for? Did she live a double life—the demure, irreproachable Countess of Brampton in public, a high-class little whore in private? No, that must be going too far. He passed a shaking hand across his forehead. There could not be that much duplicity in her. It was his Meg he was thinking of! But then, half an hour before, he would not have dreamed it possible for Meg to dress up and act like his little French angel. My God, that was Meg he had made love to!

Brampton closed his eyes and tried to force his whirling thoughts into some order. A loud cracking sound brought his eyes open again. The fan lay in two pieces in his hands. He tossed them on top of the other contents of the box and pulled himself wearily to his feet.

Meg! His angel! His wife! His hopes for a beautiful marriage had died in the last half-hour. The woman he had loved and longed for did not exist. There was only a woman he did not know. Physically, he knew her intimately. And they had shared the same home for several months. But he did not know her. He had married her so that she would bear his heirs. And after amost daily intimacies, there was no sign of a pregnancy. Did she know how to prevent that, too, the little schemer? Brampton laughed harshly and returned to his own room, leaving the box of clothes open on his wife's bed.

He lay down on his bed, though for many hours he did not close his eyes. He fell into an uneasy doze at dawn and awoke in a foul mood and with a crashing headache when Stevens brought him his shaving water and pulled back the heavy draperies from the windows.

There could be no continuation of business that day. Brampton wrote hasty notes to his man of business and the engineer he had hired, instructed his valet to pack his bags and have his curricle ready to leave in one hour's time, and proceeded to dress himself and eat what breakfast he had appetite for.

He was on his way a little before the appointed time. He estimated that he should be at Brampton Court soon after the luncheon hour. What a different homecoming he was contemplating this morning, though, from the one he had looked forward to yesterday. Then he was going home to his perfect Meg, his little porcelain doll, to try, ever so gently, to win her love. Now he was going to confront a bold, two-faced little schemer with her duplicity, to demand an explanation, to mete out punishment. She was certainly going to discover how hard his hand could be before he decided which of his estates would serve as the most cheerless place of banishment for her.

* * *

The Earl of Brampton drove his curricle into the courtyard of his country home through a drizzle that seemed to herald a heavier rain later on. It suited his mood to perfection, he thought grimly, making no attempt to prevent droplets of rain from dripping off his hair and down the back of his neck. He jumped down from his high perch, handed the ribbons to a groom who had come running from the stables, and glanced up to the windows of the drawing room as he ran up the steps and into the house.

"Where is her ladyship?" he asked the footman who took his damp hat and gloves.

"The countess is not at home, my lord," the footman replied, his voice expressionless, his posture stiff. There had been some gossip belowstairs about the goings-on of the morning, and he did not at all like the sound of his lordship's voice or the expression of his face.

"My mother?"

"The dowager Countess of Brampton is in her room, I believe, my lord."

"Thank you." Brampton took the stairs two at a time and knocked on his mother's door. Perhaps she would know where he could find his wife. He was in no mood to postpone this confrontation until she chose to put in an appearance.

"Enter," his mother's voice said from inside the room. She was reclining on a chaise longue, a lace handkerchief held delicately to her forehead. Her lady's maid stood behind her, holding her vinaigrette.

"Ah, Richard, my dear," she said languidly, "thank heaven you are home."

"What is it, Mama?" he asked, his brows knitting. The dowager paused in the middle of her big scene and surveyed her son. He was obviously blue-deviled over something. He could not have heard yet, though, surely, or he would not be standing so still in the doorway. It flashed through her mind that marriage had not brought much happiness to her favorite son. And yet Margaret was a gem of a wife, even if she was not as flashy and elegant as some of the girls of the *ton.* And why had there been no announcement of the impending event? Her woman's intuition told her that such an occasion was less than nine months away. Was he not pleased? Had Margaret not told him for some reason? The boy needed a good jolt to convince him of what a treasure he was ignoring. And how dare he barge into her room looking as black as thunder when she was the one with all the woes? She decided on impulse to play devil's advocate.

"It's Margaret," she said faintly.

"Meg?" Was that a look of alarm that momentarily flashed into his eyes. "Is she ill, Mama? Hurt? Where is she?"

"Gone!"

"Gone? What are you talking about, Mama?" The earl strode impatiently into the room and stood over the wilting form of his mother.

"Gone to Portsmouth, Richard. Don't ask me why, my dear."

"Why in thunder has she gone to Portsmouth, Mama? You make no sense at all. Who accompanied her?"

"Devin Northcott, Richard."

"Dev? Why?" Brampton had gone very still.

"Betty, my vinaigrette, please!" The dowager waved a hand vaguely in the direction of her maid. "I think maybe you should go after them, Richard."

Brampton stood rooted to the spot for a moment.

"When did they leave?" he asked with dangerous calm.

"Maybe half an hour ago, dear," she said.

Ten minutes later, the earl was galloping through the gates of Brampton Court, having taken time only to change into a dry coat and to saddle his fastest horse. But already he was soaked.

Margaret rose to her feet as Brampton stood in the doorway of the private parlor at the Crown and Anchor Inn. Devin's hand stayed on her shoulder.

"Richard!" she cried. "What brings you here?" But the glad smile died from her lips as she realized that he was not looking at her. He stood, dripping rainwater onto the carpet, his blue eyes arctic, gazing at Devin.

"I shall see you outside, Northcott," he said very quietly. "Now!"

"I say, Bram," Devin said awkwardly, and he removed his hand from Margaret's shoulder as if he had suddenly realized that it was still there, "you ain't annoyed, are you?"

"I suggest you move immediately," Brampton said through his teeth. "I should hate to make a scene inside a public inn in the presence of a *lady*!"

"Hey, Bram." Devin was beginning to flush with anger. "You've no call to be on your high ropes, y'know. I had to bring lady Bram with me. Wasn't much choice, old man."

"Out!" Brampton said. His eyes had not once shifted from Devin's.

"Richard," Margaret began, "I think there has been some misund—"

"Silence, ma'am!" he thundered, his eyes still not shifting, his voice cold as ice. "You will remain here until I come for you, and silent until I speak to you."

Margaret's face turned chalk-white and she swayed noticeably to her feet. She put a shaking hand to her mouth.

Devin's eyes narrowed. "Can't have you talk like that to a lady," he said. "even if she is your wife. Let's go, Brampton!"

The earl stepped to one side to allow his adversary to pass through the doorway ahead of him. Devin almost collided with Charles, who came bouncing in.

"Anxious to get going, Northcott?" Charles asked cheerfully. "Are the other ladies not down yet? Hey, Dick, where did you spring from?" He stopped in momentary amazement and then burst into amused chuckles. "Who's next?" he said. "Mama and the three girls? We should have quite the family gathering by nightfall."

"What the devil is going on?" Brampton's fists were clenched at his sides. He was regarding Charles as intently as he had looked at Devin just a few minutes before.

"Well, I'm trying to get my betrothed transported from this inn to Brampton Court by nightfall, Dick. But the party keeps getting larger and larger, you see. If I wait much longer, I shall need a whole caravan of carriages." He grinned at the three occupants of the room and then eyed each of them more penetratingly. "Hey, do I detect a certain tension in the air?"

"I believe your brother has just made the same error about me as I made about you when I arrived," Devin said stiffly.

"He thinks you're eloping with Charlotte?" Charles grinned. "Well, that would be more like it, I would say." He winked at Margaret, but suddenly found himself lunging forward to catch her as she fell. "By Jove, Dick," he said, glancing up at his brother with startled eyes as he placed her half-fainting form in a chair and chafed her hands, "you didn't believe what I think you believed, did you?"

Brampton had not moved, had made no effort to go to the assistance of his wife.

"I think you had better start explaining some things, brother," he said quietly.

"Again?" Charles asked, pained. But he was saved from an immediate explanation by the arrival in the room of Charlotte, Juana, the second cousin, and the duenna.

"We are ready," Charlotte announced gaily. "It is amazing how quickly one can learn sign language. Charles, introduce Juana to my sister."

Juana meantime was also chattering to Charles, perhaps saying the same thing in Spanish.

"Oh, my lord!" Charlotte said, suddenly noticing her brother-in-law standing silent to one side of the door. "Are you here, too?"

"I believe I took a wrong turn somewhere on the road," he said grimly. "I seem to have walked into Bedlam."

It took Charles another precious ten minutes to explain the situation to everyone's satisfaction and to introduce Juana to the earl and the countess. Brampton looked somewhat dazed. Charles was not sure whether all this unexpected mixup was working to his advantage or not. Certainly his foreign bride-to-be seemed to have been accepted without argument. Perhaps he was not to escape so lightly after all, though.

"Your strange behavior seems to have caused an extraordinary degree of trouble and misunderstanding," his brother said with a calm that Charles distrusted. "We shall discuss it further at home,

Charles, when we can have more privacy. For now, I suggest that we begin the journey home if we wish to arrive before morning!"

It was agreed, after much voluble discussion in two languages, that the three Spaniards would travel together in one carriage with Charles, their servant on the box with the coachman, and that the countess would travel in the other carriage with her sister and Devin Northcott. Devin's insistent offer to ride Brampton's horse so that the earl could travel with his wife was just as persistently declined.

Brampton, Devin, and Margaret were the last to leave the parlor.

"I owe you an apology, Dev," Brampton said stiffly. "I made an unforgiveable assumption. Forgive me?"

"Don't mention it, old man," Devin replied awkwardly, and glanced uneasily at Margaret, who still sat, pale as a ghost, in her chair by the fire. He followed the others outside.

Brampton crossed the room to his wife's side. She waited, with lowered eyes, for his apology, for an end to this terrible nightmare. He had never spoken harshly to her before.

"I shall escort you to your carriage, ma'am," he said, his voice devoid of all expression, and extended his arm to her.

Margaret never knew afterward how that interminable journey was passed. The atmosphere in the carriage was almost unbearably uncomfortable. Each of the three occupants felt embarrassed in the presence of the others. Margaret herself felt humiliated that Devin had witnessed the set-down Richard had given her and embarrassed that he could have thought she was running away with Devin; she felt vexed with Charlotte. Devin was equally embarrassed at Brampton's mistake, and unhappy over the continued coolness of Bram to his wife, which had been evident when he handed her silently into the carriage; he felt shy with Charlotte, unable to say what he wanted to say because Margaret was there, and yet quite incapable of talking about other matters. Charlotte was self-conscious in the presence of Devin, unsure of his attitude toward her and therefore uncertain of how she should behave; she felt guilty in the presence of Meg, knowing she had behaved disgracefully and somehow aware that she had brought Meg into disfavor with his lordship.

The Earl of Brampton, who had been on the road all day long and who was soaked to the skin, rode close to the two carriages more by instinct than by conscious effort. His mind was almost numb. He had been humiliated by his foolish gaffe back at the inn. It had been stupidity to assume that Dev and his wife were running away together. Dev had ever proved a loyal friend and his scheming little wife had nothing to gain either socially or financially by running away. Yet he was aware that his confrontation with her was still to come. But it was going to be more difficult now that the momentum had gone from his attack. Why the devil had he wanted to scoop her up into his arms and cradle her head against his shoulder when she sat so pale and still back at that infernal inn?

And then there was Charles' situation to be dealt with when they got home. No one but Charles would be capable of presenting his family with such a surprise and in such a ludicrously mismanaged way. It was *almost* amusing, the earl decided grimly. He was going to have to contend with his mother's fits of the vapors for what would be left of the evening by the time they arrived back, he did not doubt.

Charles meanwhile was enjoying every moment of the trip, sitting beside his Juana and holding her hand, and entering into a hearty quarrel with her over the reception she had received from her future brother- and sister-in-law. She had considered it decidedly cool. He had thought it remarkably warm.

Some time after a very late dinner, when all the participants in the Portsmouth fiasco plus the dowager countess were in the drawing room trying to hold a conversation in two languages, with Charles and—to a lesser degree—the earl acting as interpreters, Devin Northcott crossed to Charlotte's side.

"These are family matters that do not concern you or me," he said quietly. "Shall we withdraw?"

She was on her feet in a moment, nervously aware that her future was about to be decided one way or another.

He led her to the library, the weather being still too damp to permit a stroll in the garden. Charlotte seated herself on a sofa; Devin crossed to the empty fireplace and rested one arm on the mantel.

"Ain't going to make a speech," he said. "You'll find some reason to bite my head off again if I do. Do I have any hope, Charlotte?"

"Any hope, sir?" Charlotte was alarmed at how loudly her voice came out.

"I love you," he said. "Want to marry you."

"Oh!"

"Oh? Nothing more to say? Most unusual."

Charlotte got shakily to her feet. "I thought perhaps I had so disgraced myself today," she said humbly, "that you would not wish to associate with me anymore."

"Well, you do get into more scrapes than any other

girl I ever knew," said Devin unwisely. "Thought I might help keep a firm hand on you. Wouldn't want m' wife jauntering around the country with other men whenever she wanted, y'know."

"Oh! There you go again," Charlotte flared. "So I am still a flirt! Still a little girl who needs a strong hand. And you, sir, are still stuffy and conceited and—oh! What are you doing?"

"Shutting you up," he said grimly. "Don't intend to have a scold for a wife."

Charlotte found herself being firmly held and soundly kissed by her stuffy, conceited suitor, and thoroughly enjoying the ordeal.

Devin was slightly breathless when he finally released her mouth. "Anything else to say?" he asked severely.

"No, Devin."

"Good."

He kissed her again, and her arms found their way around his neck and into his hair.

"Nothing official, mind," he said several minutes later as they sat together on the sofa, though they might as well have chosen a chair for all the space they occupied. "Have to leave in the morning to visit your father. Is he likely to approve?"

"Oh, I think so," she sighed, burrowing her head into his shoulder. "Will you be gone long, Devin?"

"Only as long as I have to," he said. "Probably find you gone to fight Napoleon in Spain by the time I get back."

"No, truly, Devin, I shall be waiting for you. I have loved you forever, I promise."

"Make sure it stays that way," he commanded sternly.

"Yes, Devin."

16

MARGARET WAS SITTING at her dressing table, dressed
in her white nightgown, high at the neck and long
sleeved. Kitty was unpinning her braids in preparation for brushing them out and replaiting them for
the night.

She had been so looking forward to Richard's
return home, had missed him so much in his few
days of absence. And now Lottie's stupid behavior
had spoiled everything. Oh, it was most vexing!
Margaret had been perfectly aware that it was not
quite the thing for her to ride to Portsmouth in a
closed carriage with Devin Northcott, but really,
given what they had believed, there had been no
choice. Devin himself had seen that, and there was no
more high stickler than he. Surely Richard would
have understood, too.

Margaret remembered with an inward shudder the
look on his face when he had entered the parlor and
spoken to Devin, and she remembered his words to
her. She could not understand why he had behaved
that way. Apparently there had been some misunderstanding with his mother, so that he had ridden all
the way to Portsmouth believing that she had run
away with Devin. But surely, once he had realized
the truth, he should have changed toward her. He
had begged pardon of Devin. Yet to her he had been

coldly formal ever since. He had hardly looked at her since their return home and had talked to her only when strictly necessary. She could understand that he must be embarrassed by his own mistake, but surely he owed her some sort of apology.

She realized that this evening had not been an easy time for him. Charles had done a mad thing to keep secret his betrothal and then to bring his fiancée to England to spring quite unexpectedly on his family. Juana's arrival at Brampton Court would have been a trying ordeal at any time, but under the circumstances, it had been a very exhausting evening. The dowager had, predictably, swooned quite away when first presented with her future daughter-in-law. It had taken the combined efforts of Margaret, Charlotte, Betty, and Juana's duenna to restore her to her senses.

After that the evening had proceeded as well as could be expected. In fact, the dowager showed every sign of taking a liking to the very handsome Spanish girl. She even remarked that Juana was just the sort of girl Charles needed, someone to keep him on his toes, so to speak. The young lovers had had yet another quarrel during the evening when Charles—with very obvious intentions—wanted to show her the family picture gallery, and she preferred to stay and talk to his mother, with him as translator.

Richard had been very busy trying to cope with the situation. He had conversed with the second cousin and with Juana herself in the Spanish he had acquired during an assignment with the Foreign Office. Margaret realized that he had not had the leisure to make things right with her, even if he had wanted to.

She consoled herself with that thought. Perhaps he

would come to her tonight and they would talk. He would say he was sorry for the harsh words he had spoken; she would tell him about the baby. Then he would come to her bed for a precious few minutes before retiring to his own room.

The connecting door to the dressing room opened after the briefest of taps and Richard stood there, still dressed in shirt and breeches. He had removed his coat and neckcloth. Margaret's eyes met his in the mirror. He had never come this soon after her retiring. He had never come to her before she was in bed. She felt a little shiver of fright. His eyes were as cold a blue as they had been that afternoon.

"You may leave, Kitty," he said, holding out his hand for the brush she was using. "I shall finish that."

Kitty looked inquiringly at her mistress.

"Yes, it is all right, Kitty," she said with practiced calm. "Good night."

"Good night, my lady," Kitty said, "my lord." She handed over the brush and bobbed a curtsy.

Brampton drew the brush through the full length of his wife's hair. Margaret sat very stiff and still, unable to understand her husband's mood.

"I always wondered what color it was," he murmured, half to himself, it seemed.

Margaret looked puzzled. "You mean, how long it was, Richard?"

He looked briefly but deeply into her eyes in the mirror.

"No, I knew that it waved to your waist," he said deliberately.

Margaret lowered her eyes. He was talking in riddles. He continued to brush her hair, gently at first, but with firmer strokes as the silence stretched. Finally she winced away from him.

"Richard, you are hurting me," she said.

"Am I?" He tossed the brush with a loud clatter onto the dressing table and pulled her to her feet with one hand on her upper arm. "Let us try this instead."

He jerked her around to face him and crushed her body hard against his with one ungentle arm while the other hand held the back of her head. His mouth came down to cover hers, open and demanding. Margaret surged against him, her arms encircling his neck. She responded eagerly until it became very clear that the embrace was meant to be punishing, insulting. His tongue played with hers until he had lured it inside his lips; then he sucked it into his mouth and bit down on it, until Margaret was pushing wildly against his chest, in a panic of pain and bewilderment.

She was sobbing in fright when he raised his head and looked down at her, a bitter smile raising one corner of his mouth. "Richard, what have I done?" she wailed. "Was it so wrong of me to go with Mr. Northcott this afternoon?"

He laughed. "You travel about London alone; why not about the countryside, *angel*?"

Her eyes widened in horror as she stood, still imprisoned by his hands. "Oh," she whispered, "you know!"

He laughed again into her face before flinging her from him so that she staggered against the stool. "Yes, I know," he said. "You should have burned the evidence, my dear, if the game was over. But perhaps the game was over only for me? Have you found someone else for whom to masquerade?"

"Richard, please!"

"I must admit, ma'am, it was a beautiful scheme. You could have devised a better plan for showing me how much you hate and despise me. What a fool you made of me!''

Margaret moved toward him, one trembling hand stretched out to touch his arm. He flinched away. "Richard, it was not like that," she said. "Please let me explain."

"Your behavior needs no explanation, ma'am," he said. "It is all too painfully obvious. I might as well wear a motley suit and bells! I certainly made a ludicrous picture, did I not, creeping out of the house in disguise to meet my own wife, bedding her in a friend's house, parting before dawn? You should be an actress, my dear. That final parting scene was most affecting. You made me cry, did you know that? And did you cry with laughter on the way home?"

Margaret had her face hidden behind her hands. Her shoulders were shaking. "Let me explain," she sobbed.

"I loved you, Meg," he said harshly. "I thought you were perfection. I thought myself unworthy of you."

She looked up at him with huge, tear-filled eyes.

"And all the time you were a scheming little slut," he sneered. "Was it not exciting enough to ask your husband to give you pleasure in your marriage bed? Did you have to get your thrills by pretending to have a grand and passionate affair?" His eyes narrowed. "Would you be excited if I took you now, angel, when you know that I hate and despise you as much as you did me?"

Margaret backed away from him until her back was against a wall. She had one hand pressed to her mouth to try to muffle her convulsive sobs.

He stopped a short distance away from her, the sneer still on his face. "Relax, angel," he said soothingly. "I did not come here to bed you. I came to beat you."

Margaret shook her head.

"I will not tolerate a wife whom I cannot trust," he said, his eyes narrowed again, the sneer gone.

They stood and stared at each other for timeless moments.

Margaret took her hand away from her mouth. Her face had hardened, Brampton noticed.

"If you are going to beat me, Richard," she said, her eyes on his chin, "you had better make sure that you hurt only me and not our child."

He looked searchingly at her. "You cannot bluff your way out of this, my dear."

She looked directly into his eyes, her own suddenly blazing. "You are going to beat me," she said with scorn. "What a wronged and righteous husband you are, my lord." She pushed herself away from the wall and brushed past him. In his surprise, he let her go.

"You are so indignant because I kept up a deception and met you in the way I did?" she said, turning and glaring at him. "I am a slut, my lord? Then what does that make you? At least I knew it was my own husband I was creeping away to meet. I have never been unfaithful to you, even for one moment, even in my thoughts. But you! You lied to me and stole away to meet a women you thought to be a stranger and made love to her. You were unfaithful to me, Richard. But that does not matter, does it? Men are permitted such lapses. You are a hypocrite, my lord. You live by a double standard."

"Meg," Brampton said, trying to stop this angry tirade, which he could not quite believe was coming from his wife.

"No, I have been quiet too long," she said, her eyes flashing at him. "Have I made a fool of you, my lord? Maybe I could be forgiven, even if that had been my intention. Could anything be more humiliating than the way you have treated me? I knew you made a marriage of convenience with me. I did not expect love. But you did not show any feeling for me at all. On our wedding night, you knew I was an innocent, you must have known that I was frightened. And yet you just—you just *used* me. It was horrible, my lord, humiliating. I felt like a thing!''

"Meg,'' he said, moving toward her and reaching out his hands. "Please! I never meant—''

"Well, now you can go ahead and beat me,'' she said with bitter defiance. "I don't care anymore. Are you going to use your bare hands, my lord, or do you have to return to your room for your whip? If your child survives, Richard, I shall have done my duty, at least. And that is all you ever wanted of me, is it not?''

"Meg, my dear,'' he begged, putting his hands firmly on her shoulders, "please stop this. Stop hurting yourself.'' His eyes, she noticed in some surprise, were brimming with tears. One spilled over and rolled down his cheek as she watched. Without thinking, she reached out a hand and brushed it away.

"Richard,'' she whispered.

They stared at each other, eyes wide with tears. Brampton pulled her against him and held her head against his shoulder.

"Meg, my sweet,'' he whispered against her hair, "have I wronged you so much? I had no idea you felt so strongly, my love.''

"No, most people do not,'' she mumbled into his shirt.

He kissed her temple gently; she turned her head until their lips met.

"Richard, love me, please love me,'' she begged against his mouth.

And then she could say no more. His mouth opened over her to block out more words and his tongue was plunging deeply over hers. He crushed her body against his. Heat rose between them as her arms went up to twine around his neck.

"Meg, my little angel," he groaned, hot lips against her neck and her throat, hands twining in her thick hair.

And then he was pulling at her nightgown, tearing off some buttons in his haste to remove it. Margaret gasped and came against his length again, naked this time. He bent and lifted her into his arms and carried her to the bed. He leaned over her, drinking in the sight of her, from her passion-filled eyes and parted lips, over the perfect breasts and tiny waist, wrapped in her own hair, over the slightly rounded stomach and soft thighs, down to her tiny feet.

"God, you are so beautiful," he said unsteadily, standing to remove his own clothes.

Margaret shivered at the sight of his hard-muscled body and at the touch of his hands when he joined her on the bed, gentle at first, but seeking out unerringly the places that would make her body hum with passion. He took her hand in his, watching her through half-closed lids, and placed it against his chest. And for the first time, she began a slow and shy exploration of his body, gradually emboldened by his gasps of desire.

Thoroughly aroused by her touch, he rose up and toppled her onto her back and came down hard on top of her. Control snapped for the moment, he crashed into her, calling her name and continuing to caress her with his hands.

Margaret too cried out and arched her hips upward in order to receive him more deeply. He moved firm hands to her shoulders—a familiar

gesture—as he taught her his rhythm. But there was
nothing purely businesslike about this lovemaking
He began with slow, shallow strokes that teased her
hips into grinding rhythmically into his, which had
her panting and pleading for more.

The depth and the tempo of his thrusts increased
gradually to answer her need. When he finally felt
her muscles tighten and strain against him in mute
appeal for release, Brampton lifted his head and
gazed down at her until she opened her eyes.

"This is all for you, Meg, my wife," he said, and he
thrust and held deep inside her until he felt her
shudder into release and saw a look of surprise and
wonder glaze her eyes. He withdrew and thrust once
more, his face in the hollow of her neck, and
descended with her into a world of total peace.

They clung together damply while their hearts
slowed to normal beat, and then Brampton rolled to
one side of her, his arms still circling her warm little
body. They lay with eyes closed for several minutes

"Tell me now, Meg," he said finally, brushing her
lips with his and tightening his hold on her shoulder
"Tell me about it, my little angel."

"I loved you," she said. "I loved you so much for
six years. When I used to see you and you did no
notice me, I thought I could not bear it. But when
did not see you, it was even worse. And when you
came to Papa and asked me to marry you. I told
myself that you did not love me, that you just needed
a wife and an heir. I told myself and told myself, bu
it still broke my heart, Richard, when I knew for
certain."

He held her very close and laid his cheek on her
head while her hair cascaded over his arms.

"And then I couldn't stand it anymore and I told

Charlotte. And she persuaded me to dress up again as I had when we first met. I knew it was madness, Richard, but I just once wanted to see you look at me as you did when I was eighteen. Just once I wanted to know that you wanted me."

"Meg, my sweet love, why did you not just tell me?" he asked.

"How could I, my lord? I might have ended up looking very foolish, and embarrassing both myself and you."

"Oh, my little darling!"

"And then, after that first time, I couldn't stop," she said. "I wanted you so badly, Richard. You are a man. You could turn to a woman whenever you wanted. But I am a woman. I lived with dreams for six years and then I lived with disappointment. I did not mean to make you feel foolish, my lord, indeed I did not. I came to you only because I wanted you and needed you. And when you said good-bye, Richard, it was as painful for me as it was for you. I thought I would never know you in that way again." She buried her face against his shoulder.

"Meg, will you forgive me?" he whispered into her hair.

One arm crept around his neck and he had his answer.

"Is it true about the baby, little one?"

She nodded against his shoulder.

Suddenly Brampton leapt out of the bed and reached down to lift her into his arms.

"What are you doing?" she asked against his neck.

"I am taking my wife to my bed," he said decisively. "And that is where she belongs every night and all night for the rest of our lives."

He carried her through to his bedchamber and set

her down on his bed, where she had never been before. He looked down at her, a smile in his eyes as he got in beside her.

"I thought I knew you, Meg," he said. "And thought I loved my sweet, quiet little wife. I think am going to love the little fireball just as well."

"Do you truly love me, Richard?" she asked wistfully.

"What words will convince you?" he asked, propping himself on one elbow and cupping her face with his other hand. "I love you, my darling, my love, my sweetheart, my angel."

She smiled her rare smile. "That's nice," she said.

"I think I am ready to show you my feelings again," he said, and grinned. "Actions speak much louder than words sometimes, do you not agree?"

"I would never disagree with my husband," she said demurely.

He chuckled. "I shall remind you of that, ma'am, next time you are yelling at me and looking as if you are ready to throw things."

"Ah, but we must make sure there is no next time, monsieur, *n'est-ce pas?*" she said huskily before his mouth silenced her again and his hands went to work on her.

About the Author

Raised and educated in Wales, Mary Balogh now lives in Saskatchewan, Canada, with husband, Robert, and children, Jacqueline, Christopher, and Sian. She is a school principal and an English teacher.